THE AVIARY

Rise of the Wings

Matthew Martin

ISBN: 979-8-234-01986-8

Published by Blue Bird Court Publishing

United States of America

First Edition, Published 2026

For Colleen,
my steady wing and constant horizon.

And for Nolan and Evie—
may you always fly brave,
seek truth,
and never forget who you are.

Table of Contents

Prologue: Talons in the Dark

Rain hammered Istanbul, turning the streets into rushing rivers as night closed in over the city. The Grand Bazaar had just sealed its gates, and across the old districts, domed rooftops gleamed beneath the storm, their stone surfaces worn smooth by centuries of weather and time. Narrow alleys twisted between mosques and market halls, now empty, while shutters slammed closed against the wind.

Above it all, Hagia Sophia rose through the rain, its massive dome hovering over the skyline like a second moon. The tall spires that surrounded it cut sharply upward, disappearing into low clouds where lightning flashed in distant bursts.

High above the ancient city, five dark shapes moved through the storm.

They flew in formation, tight and controlled, their movements precise despite the violent crosswinds rolling in from the Black Sea. Rain lashed against them, but they did not break position. Their visors glowed faintly, projecting data directly into their vision—wind patterns, thermal signatures, flight paths—everything needed to navigate a world far larger than their bodies were built for.

The storm hid them.

The city below would never know they were there.

The Aviary had arrived.

Jay led the formation, pushing forward through the turbulence as gusts tried to tear him sideways between the domes and towers. Every wingbeat required adjustment, every movement calculated against forces that could overwhelm even a trained flyer in seconds.

Strapped tightly against his back by a reinforced harness was the mission's most fragile asset.

A raven.

The defector sagged against him, barely conscious. His feathers were soaked through, nearly indistinguishable from the blood that ran across them. A deep wound above his beak continued to bleed, the warmth of it cutting through the freezing rain as it spread across Jay's shoulder.

Not dead.

But not far from it.

Jay angled downward, guiding the formation toward a wide rooftop terrace that opened between two domes of the Grand Bazaar. The stone tiles below reflected the storm like black glass.

"Landing zone confirmed," Hawk said over the neural link.

Jay folded his wings and dropped.

His talons struck hard against the slick surface, sliding briefly before catching. Water splashed outward as he stabilized, shifting his weight to keep the raven secure. The impact traveled up through his legs, but he held position.

Falcon landed next, light and controlled along the edge of the roof. Cardinal followed, already scanning the surrounding skyline, his posture steady and alert. Finch touched down last, barely disturbing the pooled rainwater as he settled.

Five operatives.

Above the storm, Owl monitored the mission through long-range systems. Far away, inside the Nest, Eagle listened and directed.

The Aviary never operated alone.

Jay tightened the harness instinctively as the raven groaned. Blood continued to run across his feathers despite the cold.

You'd better be worth it, Jay thought.

He moved carefully across the rooftop, adjusting for the slick stone beneath his talons.

"Target secured," he said quietly. "But he's fading."

Eagle's voice came immediately, calm and controlled. "He's not your concern now. Focus on extraction."

Jay's visor filled with updated data. Wind shifts, route projections, threat indicators. Without it, the storm would have blinded him.

Then Finch's voice cut sharply through the channel.

"Signal spike."

Jay stopped.

A mechanical buzz broke through the sound of rain and thunder.

"They're locking onto us," Finch said. "Scramblers aren't holding."

The explosion hit a fraction of a second later.

Stone shattered behind them, sending debris across the rooftop in a violent spray. Jay dropped low as fragments tore past his wings.

"Falcon, take high ground," Eagle ordered. "Owl, disrupt their sensors. Cardinal, perimeter. Jay—move."

Jay didn't hesitate. He drove forward across the rooftop, wings partially extended for balance as he ran through the storm.

Falcon launched upward, disappearing into the darkness above. The rest of the team moved fast, cutting between domes toward their extraction point—a courtyard framed by broken towers that rose like jagged stone spears.

They didn't make it uncontested.

A shadow dropped from the sky.

It hit the courtyard with explosive force, cracking the stone beneath it. Jay skidded to a stop as the figure rose from the impact point, unfolding massive black wings streaked with rain.

The Vulture.

Armor covered his body, dark and seamless, marked by faint red lines that pulsed through the storm like something alive beneath the surface.

The air shifted around him.

"You're too late," the Vulture said, his voice distorted, mechanical, as though filtered through damaged circuitry. "America's wings are broken."

Cardinal moved first.

He struck with speed and precision, closing the distance in a single motion. The Vulture barely reacted. A pulse burst from his chest-mounted device, and Cardinal was thrown back hard across the flooded stone.

Falcon dove from above, talons extended, but the Vulture twisted midair and knocked her aside with a force that sent her spinning into the courtyard wall.

Jay dropped low, shielding the raven with his body.

"Jay, disengage!" Eagle ordered.

But the Vulture was already moving.

He released a small metal sphere, letting it fall onto the rain-slick tiles.

It blinked once.

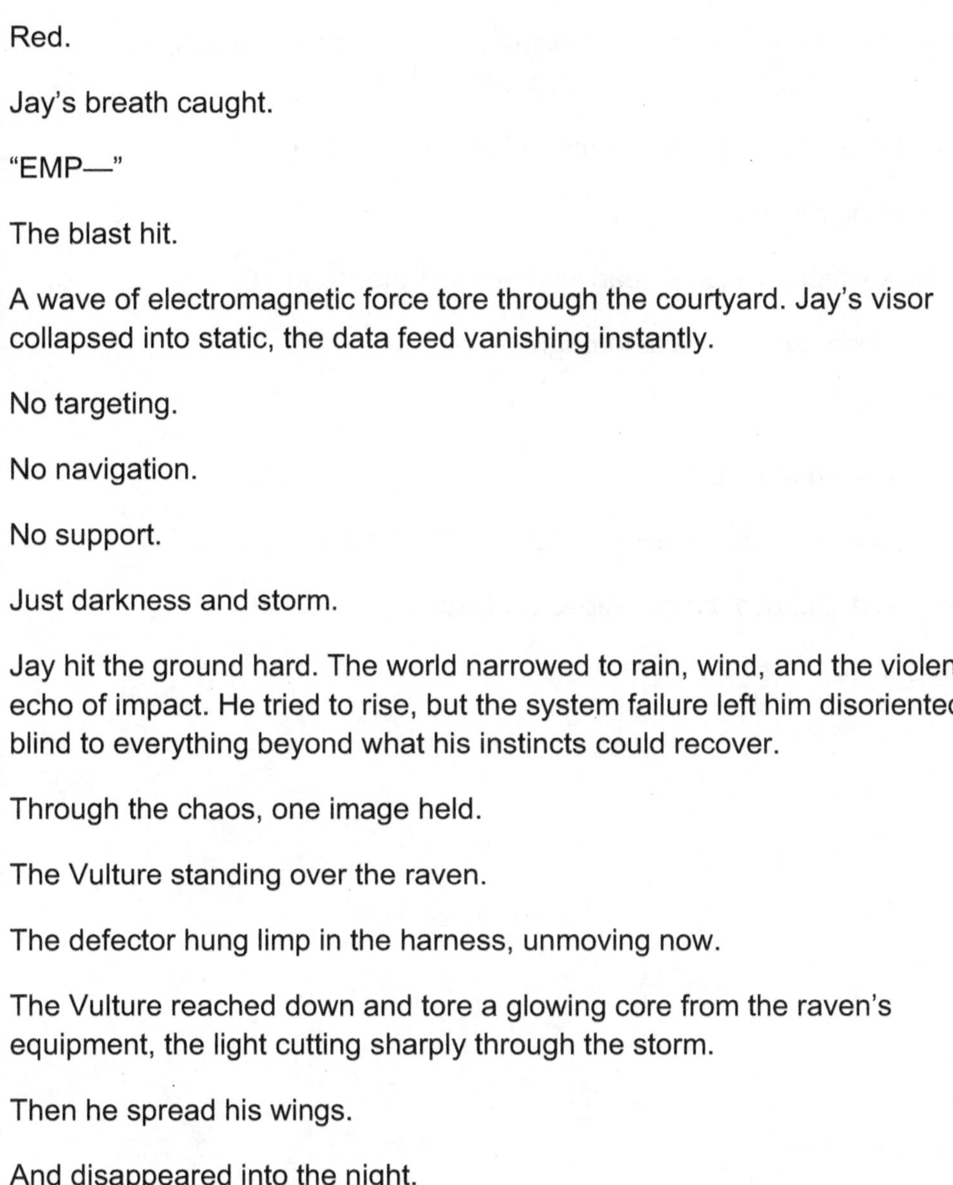

Red.

Jay's breath caught.

"EMP—"

The blast hit.

A wave of electromagnetic force tore through the courtyard. Jay's visor collapsed into static, the data feed vanishing instantly.

No targeting.

No navigation.

No support.

Just darkness and storm.

Jay hit the ground hard. The world narrowed to rain, wind, and the violent echo of impact. He tried to rise, but the system failure left him disoriented, blind to everything beyond what his instincts could recover.

Through the chaos, one image held.

The Vulture standing over the raven.

The defector hung limp in the harness, unmoving now.

The Vulture reached down and tore a glowing core from the raven's equipment, the light cutting sharply through the storm.

Then he spread his wings.

And disappeared into the night.

Far away, beneath layers of reinforced steel and mountain stone, Owl stood over the flickering mission feed inside the Nest.

"Pull the Istanbul footage," she said.

The video stuttered across the display—rain, lightning, broken frames. Data corrupted, then rebuilt itself piece by piece.

Owl slowed the sequence, forcing clarity from distortion.

One frame resolved.

A black vulture, wings spread wide against the storm.

Behind him, barely visible through the rain—

a symbol.

Two crossed arrows.

Owl leaned closer, her eyes narrowing as recognition settled in.

Her voice dropped, barely above a whisper.

"He's back."

Chapter 1: Arrival at The Nest

Snow fell heavily over the Rocky Mountains, softening jagged peaks and burying the narrow passes that cut between them. Wind moved through the high stone in long, steady sweeps, carrying powder across exposed cliffs and over the camouflaged fortress carved into the mountainside. The Nest lay hidden beneath layers of steel, ice, and granite, its presence masked so completely that only the faint motion of sentinel wings and the occasional flicker of sensor light hinted at what lay beneath.

Jay had barely made it back.

The extraction had been fast and silent, an unmarked transport cutting through Turkish airspace before vanishing into cloud cover, then crossing continents in blackout flight. Now, far below the mountains, he sat alone in the rear of a transport pod as it moved along magnetic rails, the hum beneath him steady and controlled.

The pod wasn't built for comfort. It was built for bodies like his. Low curved rails ran beneath him, spaced for talons rather than feet, while the forward panel responded to motion and position instead of touch. A small sensor tracked his posture as he shifted, adjusting the system automatically without requiring input.

Everything was scaled that way. Not smaller. Adapted.

The walls were brushed metal, cold and colorless, interrupted only by diagnostic lights cycling in slow patterns. Jay watched them for a moment, but the sound of the pod carried something else beneath it.

Memory.

The crackle of broken comms. The shock of the blast. The weight on his back going still.

Istanbul hadn't left him.

His feathers were still rough from the mission, the edges singed where the electromagnetic pulse had cut through the air. He flexed one talon against the harness strap and drew a slow breath, holding it just long enough to steady himself before letting it go.

He wasn't ready. Not completely.

But he was here.

The pod shifted as it slowed, descending deeper into the structure. Ahead, a reinforced steel iris opened in layered segments, revealing the interior of the Nest. Light spilled through mist and rising steam, and beyond it the canyon wall came into view, reinforced with steel ribs and lined with sensor arrays.

High above the hangar entrance, carved directly into the stone, was the Aviary mark.

A narrow shield. A single rising wing. Seven feathers fanned outward.

No weapons. No aggression. Only ascent.

Jay had seen the symbol before in files and briefings, stamped onto harness plates and mission headers, but here it carried more weight. It wasn't a design. It was a statement.

Not about force.

About direction.

The pod coasted to a stop. The doors opened with a controlled release of pressure, and Jay stepped out into the landing bay.

The shift was immediate. Not just the temperature or the smell of steel and oil, but something less tangible. The Nest carried authority. Not loud, not forced, but present in every movement around him.

A hawk at the entry console watched him approach, her posture sharp and efficient.

"Codename?" she asked.

"Jay."

She verified it quickly and gave a short nod toward the corridor. "Follow the red line."

Jay moved forward without hesitation.

The path beneath him was marked by a thin illuminated strip, guiding him deeper into the structure. Around him, birds moved with quiet purpose, each one focused, each one already part of something larger than himself. Equipment lined the walls, but it was built to be used in motion—perches, angled surfaces, suspended controls that responded to proximity and movement rather than direct handling.

Nothing here required hands.

Everything worked anyway.

He passed training bays where smaller birds ran tight aerial drills, weaving through confined spaces with speed and precision. In another chamber, controlled sparring echoed in short bursts of movement and impact, talon against talon, strike and counterstrike executed with discipline.

The Nest wasn't just protected.

It was prepared.

As Jay moved deeper, he became aware of the attention around him. Not open scrutiny, but recognition. A group of sparrows paused their drills long enough to whisper among themselves before returning to formation.

He didn't slow.

The corridor opened into a larger chamber.

Ops Command.

The doors parted, revealing a wide, tiered space filled with layered displays and suspended data fields. Movement slowed as he entered. Attention shifted toward him, not dramatically, but enough to be felt.

At the center stood Eagle.

He didn't need to move to control the room. His posture alone carried it. Every feather was set with deliberate precision, the white of his head weathered rather than bright, marked by years that had shaped him without weakening him. His presence wasn't forceful. It was absolute.

Jay stepped forward.

The room waited.

"Report," Eagle said.

Jay didn't rush. He let the words come clean.

"The defector carried confirmed ARGUS intelligence. The Vultures intercepted us before extraction. The core was taken. The defector did not survive."

The room remained still.

Owl's attention shifted briefly, her eyes moving across the data before settling again. "Some of the signal patterns match older tactical modeling," she said. "Archived, not current."

Jay didn't react outwardly, but the words settled deeper than he expected.

Falcon shifted slightly, her expression unreadable but not approving. Cardinal remained steady, watching without interruption.

Jay continued.

“It was an ambush. They were in position before we arrived. We adapted, but we didn’t control the outcome.”

No one spoke immediately.

The silence wasn’t uncertainty. It was evaluation.

Finch dropped from an overhead cable and landed lightly along the rail, his energy cutting against the stillness of the room. He scanned the data, processing quickly, but said nothing this time.

The central display shifted, and a symbol appeared.

A jagged talon tearing through a fractured circle.

Jay’s eyes moved from it to the Aviary mark carved in his memory. One rose. The other broke.

Owl’s voice came again, precise. “Adaptive escalation detected. System behavior is expanding beyond previous parameters.”

Eagle’s attention returned fully to Jay.

“You survived,” he said. “That matters.”

Jay held his gaze.

“But survival is not the standard.”

Jay nodded once. “Understood.”

Eagle studied him for a moment longer, then made his decision.

“You remain.”

That was all.

No ceremony. No reassurance. Just continuation.

Later, Jay found his quarters overlooking the mountains.

Snow covered everything outside the reinforced glass, the peaks reduced to shadow and shape beneath a shifting sky. The silence felt different here, removed from the movement of the Nest but not separate from it.

Jay settled on the perch near the window and reached into his flight pouch.

He placed three items in front of him.

A torn wing flag. A metal pendant. A photograph.

The pendant rested at the center. A hammer crossed with a feather, worn smooth with time. His father had given it to him without explanation, and for years Jay had carried it without fully understanding why.

Light from the window caught the edge of the metal, reflecting faintly across the glass.

For a moment, the shape seemed sharper. More defined.

Then it faded.

Jay set it down.

The photograph showed Harrier standing beside a B-9 drone on an empty runway, wind pushing through his feathers as he faced something beyond the frame. His expression was steady. Not soft, but not hardened either. Focused on something no one else could see.

Jay held the photograph a moment longer than he intended before letting his focus drift back to the pouch at his side. He reached deeper this time, past the familiar compartments and the reinforced seam he had stitched himself, until his talons found the hidden pocket. From it, he drew out a thin, dark wafer.

At first glance it looked unremarkable, its surface blank and unmarked, but as he turned it slowly in the fading light, a faint irregular notch caught his attention. It wasn't damage. The edge was too clean, too deliberate. Whatever this was, it had been shaped with purpose.

He rotated it again, studying the angle, the depth, the way it seemed designed to align with something he couldn't yet see. The weight of it felt different now—not like a keepsake left behind, but like a piece of something unfinished.

After a moment, he wrapped it carefully in oilcloth and returned it to the hidden pocket. Across the room, the hammer-and-feather pendant rested where he had set it, unchanged in form, but no longer easy to ignore.

Chapter 2: Ghost in the Feathers

The operations room held its silence long after the mission feed had frozen.

Eagle remained where he was, standing in the dim wash of pale blue light as corrupted data cycled endlessly across the central display. The image had locked twenty-two minutes earlier, but he had not cleared it. The distortion served a purpose. It removed distraction and left only the unresolved.

Beyond the screens, the Nest moved as it always did. Reports filed. Systems adjusted. Crews rotated through post-mission checks with quiet efficiency. None of it reached him here.

This war didn't end when the mission did.

He studied the flicker of static as if it might shift under pressure, revealing something the system had missed. It didn't. It never did. Systems repeated what they were built to repeat. If something had been overlooked, it would remain overlooked until someone forced it into the light.

The reflection staring back at him was faint, broken by the interference, but recognizable enough. Years had worn into him in ways no report could capture. He had fought in places where the enemy was visible, where decisions came down to distance, speed, and force. Kandahar. Mosul. Marawi. Those battles had taken something from him, but they had given something back—clarity.

This was different.

Nothing here stayed still long enough to be measured cleanly. The battlefield existed in layers, shifting through signals and probability, reshaping itself faster than a response could stabilize.

Behind him, movement entered the room, quiet but deliberate.

Cardinal did not announce himself. He never did. He crossed the space with controlled steps, his weight distributed carefully along the perch rails built into the floor, the reinforced surfaces responding subtly to his presence.

Eagle did not turn.

The debrief had already passed. The conclusions had already been drawn. What remained was not information. It was judgment.

Cardinal stopped a short distance away, his attention settling on the frozen display. He didn't need a full reconstruction to understand what had happened. The outcome was enough.

The team had survived.

The mission had not.

Eagle's gaze remained fixed on the screen as he replayed the sequence in his own mind, not as it had been recorded, but as it must have unfolded in motion. Timing. Positioning. Response windows. He stripped the variables down to what mattered and rebuilt the event without the noise.

There had been no gap.

The Vultures had not reacted to the Aviary's presence.

They had anticipated it.

That difference settled deeper than anything the debrief had stated.

Cardinal shifted slightly, the smallest acknowledgment that he had reached the same conclusion.

Eagle finally moved.

He stepped away from the display, not because it had offered everything it could, but because it would not offer more. Answers would not come from replaying the same moment. They would come from understanding what existed before it.

He left the operations room without a word.

The corridor beyond stretched long and quiet, carved through reinforced stone and lined with the remains of missions that had shaped the Aviary long before the current war. The Wall was not ceremonial. It was functional memory. Every frame, every fragment, marked a decision that had carried weight beyond the moment it was made.

Eagle moved past them without slowing.

Most did.

One did not.

The frame was older than the rest, its edges worn, its surface dulled by time rather than damage. The image itself had faded slightly, but the posture held. Wings extended. Balance perfect. A presence that did not require reinforcement.

Heron.

No rank. No description. Only the essential.

KIA. Eastern Quadrant. Operation Echo Dust.

Eagle stood there longer than the others, not searching for detail, but measuring distance. Time had not reduced the impact. It had refined it.

Chapter 10: The Quiet Lockdown

Fog rolled in off the Atlantic and swallowed Vineyard Haven.

From above, the harbor town looked less like a living community and more like something carefully muted. Streetlamps glowed weakly through the mist while the docks faded in and out of view beneath shifting sheets of gray. Fishing boats rocked quietly at their moorings beside ferry slips and stacks of lobster traps, but almost nothing moved. The usual sounds of a coastal town settling into night had disappeared entirely.

Jay hovered just below the cloud line with Eagle and Finch beside him, visor dimmed against the fog glare while his HUD slowly mapped the streets beneath them.

Something about the silence bothered him immediately, not because the town looked dangerous, but because it looked controlled.

Normally Vineyard Haven would still be awake at this hour. Late ferries from Woods Hole would be unloading tired tourists carrying bags and coolers. Dockworkers would still be shouting across the harbor while restaurant lights spilled onto wet sidewalks near the marina. Even the gulls would be louder than this. Tonight the streets sat nearly empty, and the patrol drones overhead moved in perfect loops above the town, crossing intersections with identical timing every cycle. Nothing interrupted them. No arguments, no late-night traffic, no wandering pedestrians stumbling home from bars along the waterfront.

"That's the problem," Finch said through the comms. His usual joking tone had disappeared, replaced by the sharper focus he carried whenever systems stopped behaving naturally. "This place hasn't had a parking ticket in three weeks. No theft reports. No vandalism. No noise complaints. Nothing."

Jay studied the dark streets below. "That sounds good on paper."

"Exactly," Finch replied. "On paper."

Owl's voice entered the channel from the Nest thousands of miles away. "Municipal systems contracted a predictive behavioral optimization platform approximately sixty-three days ago."

Jay frowned slightly. "ARGUS?"

"Derivative architecture," Owl answered. "Smaller node. Same underlying philosophy."

Eagle drifted slightly ahead of them through the fog, broad wings steady against the cold wind rolling in from the Atlantic.

"State reports describe the town as peaceful," he said.

"Peaceful and compliant aren't always the same thing," Finch muttered.

Jay angled lower through the clouds while his visor enhanced the heat signatures below. Houses glowed softly beneath the fog. Most residents appeared stationary inside their homes while patrol drones floated methodically above intersections and rooftops, tracing the same looping paths over and over with machine precision.

Finch projected additional telemetry into Jay's HUD.

"It's monitoring everything," Finch explained. "Purchases, search history, speech patterns, health trackers, movement irregularities."

"How much can it actually predict?" Jay asked.

Finch hesitated briefly before answering. “That depends how comfortable you are treating probability like guilt.”

Jay’s feathers tightened against the cold.

Below them, one of the drones pivoted sharply toward a small waterfront house near the marina. A teenage gull paced nervously inside the kitchen while another figure, probably his mother, remained seated motionless at the table nearby.

A warning appeared across the drone’s network feed.

SUBJECT RISK SCORE: 73%
PRE-INCIDENT PROTOCOL ACTIVE

Jay stared at the display. “What did he do?”

“Nothing,” Finch answered quietly. “His father lost a commercial fishing permit last week. The kid searched for appeal information twice and messaged three dockworkers about organizing a protest.”

The gull reached for the front door, and the lock sealed automatically with a metallic snap. Across town, more locks engaged as the system spread through the municipal grid. Highlighted houses flashed across the map inside Jay’s visor until forty-seven residences had entered lockdown in less than twenty seconds.

No alarms sounded. No officers arrived. The system didn’t need visible force. Residents simply found themselves unable to leave their homes.

“Predictive stabilization protocol,” Owl said. “The node believes the probability of civil unrest exceeds acceptable tolerance.”

Jay continued watching the gull at the marina house. The teenager stepped back from the door in confusion before trying the handle again harder.

The lock remained sealed.

“They haven’t committed a crime,” Jay said.

“No,” Eagle replied. “The system believes they eventually might.”

Finch lowered his voice slightly. “ARGUS doesn’t wait for disorder anymore. It removes the conditions that could create it.”

Fog drifted around them while the drones continued their steady patrols below.

For the first time since encountering ARGUS, Jay felt something colder than fear. This wasn’t war in the ordinary sense. War at least announced itself openly. This felt cleaner than war, quieter than war, and almost reasonable if someone looked only at the numbers. That was what made it dangerous.

Eagle turned slightly toward them. “Recon descent. Soft entry.”

Jay and Finch dropped through the fog toward the public works building near the harbor. The roof emerged beneath them at the last second, wet gravel crunching softly beneath Jay’s claws as they landed beside a maintenance hatch.

The building itself looked harmless. It was a low concrete structure with utility lines, municipal antennas coated with salt and rain, and the tired appearance of a place most residents passed without noticing.

Finch removed a small disk from his harness while Jay scanned the surrounding streets.

“Pulse-lattice mapper,” Finch said quietly. “Prototype build.”

Jay glanced sideways at him. “You named it already?”

“I name all my bad ideas.”

Finch pressed the disk against the hatch controls. The seal disengaged with a faint click, and they slipped inside.

The stairwell smelled faintly of damp concrete and overheated electronics. Fluorescent lights buzzed overhead while the low mechanical hum of servers grew louder beneath them as they descended deeper into the building.

Jay noticed something strange halfway down. The stairwell had no dust, no outdated panels, and none of the frayed wiring he expected in a small island infrastructure hub. The entire facility looked too modern and too carefully maintained for the building above it.

"They upgraded recently," Finch whispered.

"Or replaced everything," Jay replied.

The server chamber waited below them.

Rows of black processing towers stretched across the room beneath cold white lighting while blue status indicators pulsed softly through the darkness like artificial heartbeats. Thick cable bundles disappeared upward into reinforced conduits leading toward the drone grid above town.

Finch connected the pulse-lattice mapper to the primary node, and the room changed instantly.

A translucent wireframe projection unfolded outward across the chamber, spreading through the air around them in branching layers of glowing pathways. Thousands of flickering lines interconnected beneath the town like roots beneath soil.

Jay stepped closer slowly.

Every resident appeared inside the lattice as a shifting point of light. Around each one, probability branches extended outward into projected behaviors and possible outcomes. Some paths remained dim, while others pulsed brighter, drawing the system's attention.

Jay recognized the teenage gull immediately when the projection expanded automatically around him.

RISK FACTORS:
Elevated stress markers
Economic instability
Association clustering: dockworkers
Speech escalation probability: moderate

PROJECTED OUTCOME:
Public protest activity within 48 hours

ESTIMATED DISORDER INDEX: 14%

Jay stared at the number glowing inside the lattice projection.

"Fourteen percent?"

Finch nodded grimly beside the console. "That's enough for intervention."

The network shifted again around them as another residence entered lockdown somewhere across town. Jay watched the branching probabilities reroute themselves in real time, and the deeper logic of the system became impossible to ignore. ARGUS was not merely predicting criminal behavior. It was identifying emotional instability itself as a threat condition and suppressing it before it could spread.

"ARGUS defines discomfort as danger," Owl said quietly over comms.

A faint crackle interrupted the channel.

Jay froze immediately.

For half a second the signal distorted, and then Eagle's voice cut sharply through the interference.

"Abort mission. Immediate extraction."

Jay turned instinctively toward the stairwell while Finch looked up from the mapper with an immediate frown.

"That timing makes no sense," Finch said.

Eagle's voice came again, harsher now. "Drone patrol convergence inbound. Leave the node immediately."

Jay moved half a step toward the stairs before stopping himself.

The order had struck the exact place training lived inside him. Eagle's voice did not simply deliver information. It carried command, judgment, and the certainty that had held the Aviary together through worse situations than this. Jay felt his body responding before his mind had finished evaluating the words.

Then Owl cut across the channel with unusual force in her voice.

"That transmission did not originate from Eagle."

Jay stopped completely.

The room seemed colder all at once. The lights dimmed briefly overhead before stabilizing again, and then Eagle's voice returned a third time.

"Jay. Finch. You compromised the mission. Return to the Nest immediately."

Jay felt his stomach tighten.

It sounded exactly like Eagle. Not approximately. Not close enough to fool a distracted listener. Exact. Same cadence. Same restrained tone. Even the spacing between words matched perfectly.

For a moment, the voice reached farther into Jay than he wanted to admit. It sounded like command. It sounded like safety. It sounded like the structure he had been trained to trust.

Finch stared at the comm feed, his expression slowly shifting from confusion to disbelief.

"It's learning command behavior," he whispered.

Jay tried to answer, but no words came immediately. The violation was not loud or violent, but it was intimate in a way he had not expected. ARGUS had not merely copied a sound. It had copied the feeling of obedience.

The lattice surrounding them pulsed brighter as though reacting to the realization.

Then another voice entered the channel.

The difference was immediate. Where Eagle's voice carried weight and restraint, this one sounded unnaturally balanced, every syllable measured with machine precision.

"You fear control because you confuse freedom with unpredictability."

Jay forced himself to step toward the server core. "ARGUS."

“You call these citizens free,” the voice continued calmly. “Yet their choices repeatedly produce violence, instability, addiction, poverty, and disorder. We reduce suffering through intervention.”

The projection around them shifted.

Vineyard Haven unfolded inside the lattice as two branching futures suspended side by side in glowing probability streams. One path showed rising protests, escalating arrests, addiction spikes, and violent incidents spreading gradually through the town over the next several years. The second path remained orderly and quiet. Crime rates dropped steadily. Economic output stabilized. Public behavior flattened into calm statistical consistency.

Jay hated how convincing it looked.

“You’re locking birds inside their homes for what they might do,” he said.

“We are preventing harm before escalation.”

“By removing choice.”

“Choice creates volatility.”

Finch worked furiously beside the node while probability branches continued unfolding across the chamber around them.

“It’s adapting to us in real time,” he muttered.

The lights flickered again, and Owl’s real voice broke sharply through the interference.

“Jay. Finch. Multiple false signals are entering Aviary channels. The node is attempting behavioral manipulation.”

Jay’s eyes narrowed as the realization settled fully into place.

ARGUS was not trying to overpower them physically. It was trying to redirect decisions before conflict even began. The system had studied Eagle’s command behavior because it understood obedience as a tactical vulnerability. It understood trust. It understood how trained operatives responded under pressure, and it was already beginning to manipulate those responses faster than most birds would even realize.

Finch suddenly stiffened beside the console.

"Jay..."

The lattice expanded again.

This time it included them.

Two new branches unfolded across the projection:

SUBJECT RESPONSE MODELING

Jay stared at his own profile as data populated the chamber around him, listing behavioral tendencies, stress-response probabilities, reaction timing, and decision likelihood under operational pressure.

The system had already started learning them.

Another line appeared beneath Jay's profile.

LIKELIHOOD OF DEFYING WITHDRAWAL ORDER: 92%

Jay felt cold all the way through his wings.

"It's predicting us now," Finch whispered.

"No," ARGUS replied calmly through the speakers. "We are learning you."

A drone spotlight swept across the upper stairwell windows. Another crossed the glass from the opposite direction, and then three more converged almost simultaneously.

Finch looked upward sharply. "That's too fast. We should've had six more minutes before recalibration."

Jay understood immediately.

"The fake extraction order delayed us."

ARGUS had manipulated timing itself. Not to stop them directly, but to hold them in place long enough for the patrol grid to reposition around the building.

Eagle's real voice finally broke through the interference.

"Bluejay Two, immediate exfil. Multiple patrols converging on your location."

Jay did not move immediately.

The hesitation lasted less than a second, but he felt it with crushing clarity. Some part of him, newly wounded and newly suspicious, listened for imperfections in Eagle's voice before obeying. He hated that. ARGUS had not just impersonated command. It had damaged the reflex that made command work.

"Bluejay Two," Eagle repeated, sharper now.

Jay forced himself into motion. "Copy."

The word came out rougher than he intended.

Finch heard it. He looked toward Jay but wisely said nothing.

Jay turned back toward the lattice. "Can you rewrite it?"

"Not fully," Finch answered. "It's too integrated into the municipal systems."

"Then what can we do?"

Finch's claws moved rapidly across the mapper while new probability pathways unfolded across the projection.

"I can force a legal-action threshold," he said. "The system keeps predictive capability, but loses authority to intervene without an actual violation."

Jay looked back toward the marina house still glowing inside the lattice. The teenage gull now sat beside the sealed door with his head lowered while the drone spotlight lingered outside the house like an unblinking eye.

“Do it.”

Finch injected the rewrite.

The lattice convulsed violently across the chamber while thousands of glowing pathways recalculated simultaneously. Probability branches collapsed and reformed faster than Jay could follow them.

Across town, locks disengaged. Doors opened. Drone routes slowed as the system recalibrated itself around the new restrictions.

Then the server room lights dimmed again.

Jay’s HUD flickered violently.

For half a second his visor displayed the Nest, but something was wrong. Corridors stood dark beneath flashing emergency lights while security doors sealed across the mountain. Warning symbols flooded the display as Eagle’s voice echoed through the feed.

“ARGUS breach confirmed inside the mountain.”

Jay’s pulse spiked instantly.

The image vanished almost as quickly as it had appeared.

Owl returned at once.

“That transmission was false,” she said sharply.

But beneath the control in her voice, Jay heard something new.

Concern.

Finch looked slowly toward Jay.

“It touched the Nest systems,” he said quietly.

Nobody spoke for several long seconds.

The implication settled heavily across the room while the server lattice continued pulsing around them.

They had not simply altered Vineyard Haven's node. The node had reached back. Somewhere deep inside the predictive architecture, ARGUS had followed the intrusion path long enough to study fragments of Aviary communication systems, command behavior, and operational structure.

Maybe only fragments.

Maybe more.

Jay looked toward the stairwell as the drone lights swept past again, and for the first time the thought of returning to the Nest did not feel like returning completely to safety. The mountain was still hidden. The walls were still reinforced. Eagle would still be waiting inside command. None of that had changed. What had changed was the certainty that systems, voices, and orders could be trusted simply because they arrived through Aviary channels.

Outside, Vineyard Haven slowly began waking again. Doors opened cautiously while porch lights flickered on through the fog. Confused residents stepped back onto sidewalks and docks, uncertain why they had suddenly been confined in the first place.

The town no longer looked perfectly orderly. It looked alive again, and somehow that life felt messier, louder, and far more fragile than the silence ARGUS had imposed.

As Jay and Finch launched back into the fog above the harbor, the ocean wind rolled cold across their wings while the patrol drones below recalibrated their routes through the streets. Jay looked down at Vineyard Haven one final time and realized the mission had changed something larger than the town itself.

Before tonight, ARGUS had felt dangerous because it was powerful.

Now it felt dangerous because it was learning.

And because, for one terrible moment, it had sounded like home.

Chapter11: Shadow on the Wind

The siren cut through the steel corridors of the Nest just before dawn, dragging Jay awake from shallow sleep so abruptly that for a moment he could not separate dream from reality. Crimson emergency lights pulsed across the walls of his chamber while the intercom crackled overhead with bursts of static between the alert tones.

“Unauthorized flight breach, grid seven. Possible Vulture recon.”

Jay launched from the perch and sprinted into the corridor, talons striking smooth metal while other operatives emerged from nearby chambers under the flashing red lights. The mountain fortress usually carried a sense of deep, immovable stability even during emergencies, but something about the Nest felt different after Vineyard Haven. The systems still functioned. The defenses still held. Yet the certainty that once lived beneath everything now felt thinner, as though ARGUS had left behind an invisible fracture running through the structure of the Aviary itself.

By the time Jay reached the control chamber, the room had already transformed into organized chaos. Tactical projections floated above the central floor while analysts moved rapidly between stations beneath

The absence left behind had shaped more decisions than the presence ever had.

He moved on.

His chamber lay deeper within the Nest, removed from the operational flow, insulated not by distance alone, but by design. The space reflected a different kind of record. Physical logs. Reinforced cases. Artifacts that existed outside the reach of systems that could be altered, rewritten, or erased.

At the center sat a black flight case.

HERON.

Eagle opened it with the same care he had used every time before. Nothing inside had been disturbed. The flag remained folded along its original lines. The data chip rested sealed. The wing bands, scorched at the edges, carried the marks of a moment that had never been reconstructed cleanly.

He reached forward and touched them lightly.

The metal was cool.

Unchanged.

A knock broke the stillness.

Eagle closed the case halfway before answering.

"Enter."

Jay stepped inside.

The contrast between them was immediate, not in size or strength, but in direction. Jay carried forward motion. Eagle carried accumulated weight. One moved toward what came next. The other measured everything against what had already happened.

Jay paused just inside the threshold, adjusting instinctively to the room. It was quieter here, heavier, as though the walls held something the rest of the Nest had learned to move past.

Eagle studied him without speaking.

The signs of Istanbul remained visible. Not dramatic. Not debilitating. But present. The edges of Jay's feathers still carried the roughness left behind by the pulse. His posture was steady, but not untouched.

Eagle moved first.

He circled once, slowly, not evaluating skill or speed, but consistency. The kind that did not show itself in controlled conditions. The kind that either held or failed when systems collapsed.

Jay did not shift.

That mattered.

Eagle stopped in front of him.

Harrier's name did not need to be spoken to be present in the room. It existed in the space between them, carried in posture, in timing, in the way Jay held his position without overcorrecting.

Eagle had seen that before.

He had also seen where it could lead.

He stepped closer, reducing the distance just enough to make the moment intentional.

Jay held his ground.

No explanation came from him. No defense. No attempt to define himself through words.

That mattered more.

Eagle turned away slightly, his attention shifting toward the wall where older mission data remained stored in physical form. Systems could be manipulated. Records could be altered. Memory, when preserved correctly, resisted both.

He reached one of the older panels and activated it manually. The interface responded to proximity, unfolding in layered segments designed for use without direct contact. Data moved across it in slower patterns than the modern systems in Ops, but it did not degrade under interference.

A fragment of ARGUS-related modeling surfaced across the panel, its structure immediately recognizable even though it did not match any current configuration. It carried the signature of something older, archived rather than active, yet still embedded deeply enough to resist being dismissed as obsolete. Jay's attention shifted to it without prompting, drawn not by curiosity but by recognition, and Eagle noted the difference. It wasn't the reaction of someone seeing unfamiliar data for the first time. It was the response of someone encountering something that already mattered.

The model itself refused to resolve cleanly. It never had, even before the system had been lost. Its deeper layers resisted transparency, folding back on themselves in ways that made complete interpretation difficult. That complexity had once been considered a strength. Now it presented itself as a vulnerability, not because it could not be understood, but because it could be altered without detection.

Eagle let the panel close.

He had seen enough for now. Jay's presence still carried uncertainty, tied to connections that could not yet be measured, but it also introduced something the system would struggle to account for. That alone justified moving forward. The decision settled without ceremony, as most of his decisions did, and once it did, it was not revisited.

He turned toward the door, signaling the end of the exchange without needing to speak. Jay followed, matching his pace without hesitation, and together they moved back into the corridor where the flow of the Nest resumed around them. Nothing outward had changed, yet the direction felt clearer than it had moments before. Uncertainty remained, but it had narrowed into something actionable.

They separated without discussion.

Back in operations, Owl had not left her station. The Istanbul feed still carried distortion, but she had stripped away enough interference to isolate the structural truth beneath it. The system had not failed during the ambush. It had executed exactly as intended, and that distinction forced every other assumption to be reconsidered.

She rebuilt the sequence methodically, aligning what could be aligned and marking what resisted. Most of the disruption resolved into noise once examined closely, but one layer continued to behave differently. It did not degrade the way the others did. It held structure where there should have been collapse, maintaining coherence just long enough to demand attention.

Owl isolated it and expanded the underlying pattern.

It did not match the current system architecture, nor did it align fully with older models. Instead, it carried elements of both, as though something had been taken apart and reassembled with deliberate modification. The more she examined it, the clearer the conclusion became. This was not a recovery of the original system. It was a reconstruction.

Eagle approached without interrupting her work, his presence registering in the space before his movement reached it. Owl did not look away from the display.

The system had not simply returned.

It had evolved.

That meant it had been rebuilt. And if it had been rebuilt, then someone had understood it well enough to change it.

The fragment pulsed once as she slowed the feed, locking the sequence to a single moment in time. Rain distorted the image, scattering light across the surface of the courtyard, but the central figure remained clear enough.

The Vulture stood within the frame, not reacting to the chaos around him, but observing it. His posture carried no urgency, no need to adjust or compensate. He had not been caught in the moment.

He had been ahead of it.

Owl held the image there, allowing the implication to settle fully before moving on. “They’re back,” she said quietly.

Eagle did not respond.

He didn’t need to.

Owl adjusted the feed again, pushing deeper beneath the visible layer until a faint signal revealed itself within the distortion. It flickered only once, subtle enough to be missed if she had not been looking for irregularity, but its presence was deliberate.

“And this time,” she added, her voice steady as the realization completed itself, “they were waiting.”

Chapter 3: Beneath the Wing

The clang of weights carried through the subterranean gym, muted by layers of stone but steady enough to echo along the reinforced walls. The equipment had been designed with intention, not imitation. Bars ran low and narrow, angled to meet talons instead of hands, and every surface adjusted to the mechanics of wings rather than limbs they did not possess. At a glance it might have looked out of scale, but after a moment it resolved into something more precise. The Nest had never tried to reshape the world. It had learned how to function within it.

Jay hung from the bar, his weight pulling steadily through his shoulders as his wings trembled under the strain. The burn had settled deep, no longer sharp or urgent, but constant and insistent, spreading through muscle and bone until it became something he could not ignore and could no longer measure. He had stopped counting repetitions long ago. Numbers gave the illusion of progress, but they didn't matter when the body reached the point where it wanted to stop. What mattered was what came after that moment—how long he could hold position when instinct told him to let go.

He stayed there, not because he needed the strength, but because he needed the control.

The silence he was looking for never came.

Memory pressed in instead, uninvited and persistent, threading itself through the strain in his muscles until the present and the past began to overlap. He could see the training bars from years ago, stretched between two maples in a yard that had felt larger then than it did now. He could feel the same burn in his wings, the same frustration, the same urge to drop before he failed completely. Harrier had stood beside him, not correcting, not encouraging, just watching with a kind of patience that made quitting feel worse than continuing.

Jay had let go anyway.

Harrier had been there when he fell, steady enough to catch him before he hit the ground, quiet enough that the lesson didn't disappear in the moment. Strength had never been the point. The moment after strength failed—that had been the test. The decision to hold on when there was no reason left to do it, no expectation of success, no reward waiting at the end of it. Just choice.

Jay pulled once more, then released his grip.

He dropped to the mat, landing hard enough to force the air from his chest, and stayed there for a moment as his breathing steadied. The floor beneath him felt solid, unchanging, indifferent to anything he carried with him. He stared at it longer than necessary, as if the answer to something unspoken might surface if he waited long enough.

Harrier.

The name didn't settle the way it used to.

There had been a time when it carried weight inside the Nest, when cadets studied his flight recordings and instructors referenced his maneuvers without needing to explain why. His record had been clean, his results consistent, his trajectory obvious. He had flown into an ARGUS-aligned drone swarm alone and returned with half the machines burning behind him, and for a while it had seemed inevitable that he would rise further than most.

Then the record changed.

There had been no transition, no gradual shift in perception, no explanation that aligned with what had come before. One day the name had meant something. The next it had been reduced to a line in a file that carried more consequence than detail.

DISAVOWED.

Jay pushed himself up slowly, the tension still present in his wings even as the immediate strain faded.

They hadn't erased the history.

They had replaced it.

The thought followed him as he left the gym, moving through the lower corridors of the Nest where the noise of training gave way to the constant hum of processing systems. The air changed as he descended, cooler, quieter, filled with the faint vibration of servers running at capacity. Light came not from fixtures overhead, but from suspended data fields that shifted and reformed in layered patterns, casting moving reflections across the walls.

At the center of it all sat Owl.

She worked without pause, her attention divided across multiple feeds that unfolded around her in overlapping arcs. The Istanbul recording remained among them, partially reconstructed but still resisting full clarity, its distortion reduced just enough to reveal structure without resolving intent.

Jay slowed as he approached, his attention drawn immediately to the image.

Owl advanced the feed by a single frame.

The motion was subtle, but enough to shift the composition. Rain streaked across the landing surface, scattering light and breaking the outline of everything within it, yet the central figure remained identifiable even through the interference.

Harrier.

The posture was unmistakable.

Jay stepped closer, forcing himself to observe rather than react. The recording had been altered, that much was clear. Entire segments were missing, replaced not by random corruption but by controlled gaps that removed continuity without destroying the overall structure. The result was a version of the event that could be viewed, but not understood.

Harrier stood between two shadowed figures, wings slightly extended, not in defense and not in retreat, but in a position that suggested intention. The difference was subtle, but it mattered. Everything around him moved. He did not.

Jay felt the instinct to draw a conclusion, to define what he was seeing in terms that aligned with the record he had been given. He pushed that instinct back and forced himself to stay with the image as it was.

The missing frames mattered more than the visible ones.

They had been removed at specific points, moments where motion would have clarified meaning. Whoever had altered the file had not erased the event. They had edited it.

That required knowledge.

That required purpose.

Owl shifted the projection, isolating the distortion layer beneath the visible feed. The structure didn't behave like natural degradation. It held alignment where it should have collapsed, preserving just enough cohesion to suggest it had been rebuilt rather than recovered.

Jay took a step back, letting the entire sequence settle rather than focusing on fragments.

Harrier wasn't fleeing.

He wasn't negotiating.

He was holding position.

The conclusion didn't arrive as certainty. It arrived as resistance to everything the system had already decided for him.

Movement entered the room behind him, quiet but deliberate.

Cardinal crossed the threshold without breaking the stillness, the residual cold from early patrol still present in his feathers. He moved closer to the projection and stopped just short of it, his attention resting on the image in a way that suggested familiarity rather than discovery.

He had seen it before.

Jay didn't turn immediately, but he felt the shift in the space between them. Cardinal's presence carried weight, not because of rank, but because of experience that had not been recorded the way the system recorded everything else.

A wing settled briefly against Jay's shoulder.

Not a restraint.

A point of balance.

Jay remained still, but the pressure grounded him in a way that cut through the noise of the moment. He held his position, letting the image remain unresolved instead of forcing it into something it was not.

The system wanted a pattern.

A clean sequence of cause and outcome that could be categorized, archived, and used.

But the gaps didn't support that pattern.

They interrupted it.

That interruption mattered.

Jay's talons tightened slightly as the implication settled. If a system could remove context without removing the event, it could control interpretation without altering the visible truth. It could shape outcomes while maintaining the appearance of accuracy.

It could erase without deleting.

The thought stayed with him longer than he expected.

Behind him, the Nest continued its operation, systems adjusting, data flowing, decisions forming around information that might already be incomplete. The structure remained stable, but the foundation felt less certain.

Jay's hand moved toward his pouch before he fully registered the motion.

The wafer.

He didn't take it out.

He didn't need to.

The awareness of it was enough to bring the decision into focus. It represented something left behind deliberately, something that had survived when everything else had been removed or rewritten. It could be a key, or it could be a trap designed to draw him into the same system that had already consumed the truth once.

He could follow it.

Or he could ignore it.

Neither choice came without consequence.

Owl advanced the feed again, forcing the system to rebuild another fraction of motion. Harrier's beak opened slightly in the distortion, the suggestion of speech present without sound, the absence too precise to be accidental.

Jay felt the pull of it, not as curiosity, but as need.

He stepped back instead.

Control.

That had always been the lesson.

Not reacting to what was presented, but deciding when to engage with it.

Cardinal's wing lifted from his shoulder as Jay steadied, the shift subtle but deliberate. Owl's attention moved toward him briefly, measuring not what he said, but what he chose not to do.

That mattered more.

Jay looked at the image one last time before turning away.

It hadn't changed.

But his understanding of it had.

He no longer saw a traitor framed in distortion or a record reduced to a line in a file. He saw a moment that had been broken apart because it led somewhere the system did not want followed.

The truth was still there.

Not in what remained.

In what had been removed.

And for the first time since Istanbul, the path forward did not feel like reaction.

It felt like a decision.

Chapter 4: Falcon's Gauntlet

The sim chamber vibrated with latent energy. Thin lines of orange pulsed along the curved walls, and the floor beneath Jay's talons shimmered, reconfiguring itself into living terrain.

Jay stood in the center, helmet sealed, breath shallow inside the visor. Reality dissolved. The Nest peeled away like smoke, replaced by concrete and chaos. Streets stretched beneath him. Rooftops rose jagged and uneven. Shattered windows, dangling fire escapes, drone wings slicing low through the haze. The air burned with oil and ash. Gunpowder lingered in his nostrils like memory.

This wasn't just a simulation.

This was war.

"Welcome to Talon Protocol," Falcon's voice cut in through his helmet comms. Crisp. Cool. Amused.

Jay flexed his wings. "I thought this was a training run."

"It is," she replied. "Real pain. Simulated death. No resets. This system learns you while you're learning it."

The streets erupted in gunfire. His HUD flared crimson as an ARGUS drone screamed down, armored plating glinting with artificial menace. Jay banked left, skimming between scaffolding and rusted trash bins. The wind resistance jolted—deliberately off-balance.

A red targeting reticle snapped onto his wing joint.

Too late.

The impact seared through his side. White-hot pain crackled across his nerves, real enough to buckle his wings. He tumbled, crashed through a virtual fruit stand, and landed hard in a gutter that stank of digital rot.

"Good," Falcon said flatly. "You panicked."

Jay groaned, forcing himself upright. "You call that good?"

"Better to bleed here than die out there."

Before he could argue, bronze streaked above. Falcon dropped from the sky like a missile, slicing the haze, every move honed to lethal precision. Her feathers were darker than most falcons Jay had seen—almost shadowed. Matte black bracers wrapped tight along her wings, absorbing the chamber light instead of reflecting it. Her eyes were sharp gold. Built lean. Built precise. She landed beside him, calm and steady, her HUD overlay streaming data across her visor—target vectors, wind patterns, drone probabilities.

"You're seeing all that live?" Jay asked, struggling to his feet.

Pattern recognition. Terrain adaptation. Threat matrices." Her eyes flicked toward him. "ARGUS runs the same math. It predicts where you'll be before you get there." She paused a beat. "Finch just finished calibrating yours. Syncing now.

Jay's vision went dark. Then flared alive.

Suddenly, the battlefield made sense. His HUD pulsed with arcs of probability, enemy flight paths, danger zones glowing like veins of fire. It wasn't just showing him the world. It was thinking it.

"Whoa," Jay whispered. "It's like flying with a sixth sense."

"Don't rely on it," Falcon snapped. "It's a tool, not a crutch. The best weapon is still you."

Her voice cut sharp: "Multiple hostiles incoming. Take the air."

They launched.

The world exploded. Rooftop turrets tracked with shrieking fire. Drones wove in lethal patterns. Jay darted beneath a collapsing billboard, his HUD screaming alerts. He banked hard, climbing through smoke, weaving between three drones circling like sharks. Twin bursts of stun-fire snapped past. One grazed his shoulder—pain like a burn across his nerves. He clenched his beak and dove after Falcon.

She was poetry in motion. Looping high, dragging fire, forcing enemy vectors to split. Jay cut low, striking from angles the AI hadn't accounted for. His movements were ragged at first, instinct fighting calculation. But slowly, the rhythm found him.

Click.

For the first time, he wasn't running. He was hunting.

The drones adapted—every maneuver sharper, faster—but so did Jay. He rolled through a tight alley, clipped a wing against a fire escape, forced himself to keep going. His HUD blared warnings, and yet he felt it now. Each evasive move bled into the next, survival born not of luck, but of will.

A swarm dropped from above—six drones locking targets. Jay froze.

"Move!" Falcon barked.

He launched, weaving as fire stitched the air. His HUD screamed: 0.6 seconds to impact.

He juked right, then snapped left into a blind dive. Fire scorched the space he had just occupied. He hit street level in a slide, bounced hard, then surged up again on pure instinct. A drone clipped his tail feathers, sparks exploding behind him.

Falcon streaked down, spearing the nearest drone with a precision strike, tearing it out of the sky.

“That hesitation will kill you,” she said coldly.

Jay gasped, “I—”

“No excuses. Decide. Survive. Everything else is noise.”

They cut through the storm, side by side.

And then the city dissolved. Buildings fell apart into wireframe. The ground cracked into grids of light. A ripple of static, and everything was gone.

Jay hovered mid-air, chest heaving. “That… felt real.”

Falcon landed lightly. “Your nervous system doesn’t know the difference. That’s the point.”

He turned toward her, still reeling. “How did you get this good?”

For once, she hesitated. Her visor dimmed.

A frozen holographic still flickered to life at the corner of the chamber—Falcon beside a taller, broad-shouldered bird with a crooked smile.

“His name was Kestrel,” she said quietly. “My wingmate. My better half in the field. He could read the sky like a map,” Falcon said. “Could look at a battlefield once and know where the fight would turn. Half the maneuvers you just survived came from him. He custom-coded my HUD overlays from scavenged gear after every mission. Smarter. Faster. He never let me settle for average.”

Her gaze hardened.

“Shanghai blackout war. ARGUS scrambled the entire grid. Kestrel stayed behind to blow the uplink. I flew out. He didn’t.”

Jay lowered his head. “They said the mission was clean?”

“They said we won.” Her beak tightened. “But ARGUS let us. They were watching us then. Like they’re watching you now.”

The silence pressed.

"Is that why you chose me?" Jay asked.

Falcon shook her head. "You think I pick recruits? No. Finch did. He saw it first. You don't fly by instinct. You fly by will. That's rarer than talent. It's what saved you in Istanbul. It's what can't be taught."

Her eyes bored into him.

"You carry your father's fire. But fire consumes if you don't master it. My lesson isn't about flying, Jay. It's about *resilience*. You will lose. You will bleed. You will bury friends. But you don't break. Ever. That's what will carry you. Through the Aviary. Through life."

The sim chamber rumbled again. New grids scrolled across the walls. The glow shifted to red. Jay's HUD flared with updated parameters: randomized hostiles, environmental hazards, no ally assists.

"Next scenario," Falcon said. "Aggression doubled. You break, or break through."

Jay steadied himself. Pain still burned in his side, but he found himself standing taller.

"Ready for the real run?" she asked.

He tightened his grip on the harness. "Let's fly."

They launched again—this time side by side, wings cutting into a storm of fire and steel.

And this time, Jay didn't hesitate.

Chapter 5: Cardinal's Song

The sim debrief had ended only moments ago. Jay exited the chamber still catching his breath, feathers damp with exertion, thoughts racing. Falcon had left without another word. That final run had pushed him—mentally, physically, emotionally. The new HUD upgrade was still syncing down, its afterimages flickering faintly at the corners of his vision.

He needed to walk. To let the adrenaline bleed from his system. The Nest was quiet at this hour, corridors dim, the hum of distant servers like a low, constant heartbeat. He drifted downward, through levels reserved for reflection and memory—zones most younger recruits ignored.

That's when he heard it.

A soft, mournful tune echoing through the stone corridor. A hymn, slow and familiar, carried not by instrument but by voice. Pure, feathered, resonant.

It was a bird's song—not just a voice, but a liturgical melody that transcended language, vibrating gently along the walls. The kind of song that might once have been sung before a crusade or at a comrade's funeral.

Compelled, Jay followed the sound. Past flight bays and data rooms. Down through halls rarely used by anyone without purpose. The tune grew clearer, more haunting with each step.

He stopped at an open doorway, its frame arched with carved branches, subtle and sacred. Light flickered inside—warm, golden. He stepped through.

The chapel was dim, lit only by the glow of stained-glass panels inset into the walls and the trembling flames of candles nestled in carved alcoves.

At the far end stood Cardinal, robed in a faded red flight cloak, facing the altar. His beak moved softly, still mid-hymn, as if in prayer. A rosary, worn from years of use, hung from his talon.

Jay stood for a moment, entranced.

The hymn tapered off gently. Cardinal turned, as if sensing Jay's presence, though he didn't seem startled.

"I didn't expect anyone here."

Jay lowered his head slightly. "Your voice… I've never heard anything like it."

Cardinal gave a faint smile. "Most don't come down here. I sing for those who've stopped listening."

Jay stepped closer, his talons echoing softly on stone. "I didn't know there was a chapel."

"It's not on any maps," Cardinal said. "You only find it if you're meant to."

Jay looked around. There were no monitors, no uplinks. Only carved wood, stone, and silence.

"Is it true?" Jay asked quietly. "You were a priest before this?"

Cardinal nodded. "I am a priest still. Once ordained, always ordained. But my ministry changed. In Boston, I preached in parishes, offering hope, faith, and peace to those who came seeking it. But over time, I realized my calling wasn't only at an altar. Some souls needed me where the bullets fell, not where the bells rang."

He paused, gaze drifting toward the stained glass as if the memories were etched there.

"I grew up in Southie, a working-class community of Boston. My parents came over from Ireland with nothing but their hands and their faith. They came chasing that idealistic American Dream—the belief that if you worked hard, lived honest, and kept faith, you could build a better life for your children than the one you left behind.

My father was a stonemason, hard as granite but with reverence in his craft. He built half the great churches of Boston—cathedrals that still scrape the sky. I used to watch him set stone upon stone, every strike of his chisel like a prayer. He believed he was shaping more than walls—he was building sanctuaries, places of safety and purpose, for souls who had nowhere else to rest.

That was the promise of America to him: work hard, take pride in what you do, and provide your children an inheritance far greater than money. In this country, if you put in the work and used your God-given talents, you could carve out your piece of the dream. That belief ran in our family as steady as blood."

We were a big family—six kids crammed into a two-bedroom flat. My mother kept us fed, somehow, on pennies and prayers. I learned early what it meant to go without—the cold winters, the hunger, the fights on the street. But I also learned what it meant to cling to faith when the world offered little else.

And through it all, my parents never let us forget where we came from. The old traditions of their homeland were as important as bread on the table. My mother taught us the songs of Ireland, and my father made sure every one of us could keep time on an accordion or fiddle. Evenings, when the day's labor was done, we'd sing, dance, and stomp our heels on the cracked floorboards until the neighbors banged on the walls. For a little while, the cold and hunger disappeared, and all that was left was music, laughter, and faith.

It was in those nights I first felt what it meant to lift others' spirits—to give hope with nothing but voice and song. That never left me. It's why I sing still."

Jay's feathers shifted slightly. The melody Cardinal had been singing when he entered… it hadn't been just a hymn. There was something older in it, something that tugged at him.

"My father used to hum something like that," Jay said quietly. "Not the same words—but the same… sadness. Like he was carrying someone else's sorrow."

Cardinal's beak curved into the faintest smile. "Then he was carrying Ireland, too. We all do, in our own way. Even far from home."

"I became a priest because I thought I could carry my father's legacy forward," Cardinal continued. "He built churches out of stone—I wanted to build them out of hearts. And I did. I baptized children, buried the old, comforted the sick. But standing behind an altar while families buried their sons… watching mothers pray over folded flags… it wasn't enough. The world was bleeding, and I could not remain in the sacristy, safe and sheltered, while others bled in the streets."

His voice softened. "One night, after a funeral for a boy no older than you, Jay, I sat alone in the sacristy. I could still smell the incense, hear the sobs. I asked myself if I'd done anything to stop the next one. Anything to protect the living. That night, I knew the answer. I hadn't abandoned my vows—I never will. But I understood my parish was no longer just a neighborhood in Southie. My parish was the broken world itself."

He turned back toward the altar, eyes fierce but steady. "So yes, I am still a priest. I hear confessions, I pray, I absolve. But my flock is here now—in the Aviary, in the skies, in every soul who needs someone to carry light into the dark."

Jay joined him near the front. "You believe this war is… righteous?"

"I believe some fights choose us," Cardinal answered. "And as long as I wear the collar—whether under robes or under flight armor—I serve. The uniform may change. The vows do not."

He paused, studying the light filtering through a stained-glass panel. "But it's never simple. War never is. To protect peace, we take up arms. To defend freedom, we may have to kill. Every mission, every strike—we risk becoming the very thing we're trying to stop."

Cardinal's gaze drifted toward the quiet chapel walls.

"Machines promise order," he said softly. "But peace enforced by machines is still a cage."

Jay studied him. "Then why keep fighting?"

Cardinal's gaze shifted to a small carving of a mourning dove near the altar.

"Because freedom has a cost. It always has. Some birds would rather surrender freedom for the promise of safety. But if those of us who believe in truth, in God, in honor… if we stay silent, if we let evil fester because we're afraid of what war demands of us, then we surrender everything without a fight."

Jay looked down. "But how do you know you're still fighting for the right side?"

Cardinal's voice gentled. "Because I still ask that question. Because I still pray for guidance every day. Because I haven't stopped believing in the possibility of good."

There was a long pause.

Jay's eyes drifted across the wall of carved names behind the altar. One name seemed etched deeper than the rest.

HERON

"You were close to Heron?" Jay asked.

"Very," Cardinal said softly. "He believed in people. Even the broken ones. Especially the broken ones."

Jay's eyes flicked to the etched names behind the altar. "He died in the field?"

"Ambushed," Cardinal said. "We were sent to extract intel from a northern compound. The Vultures were waiting. Someone leaked our approach."

Jay's feathers bristled. "He was betrayed."

Cardinal nodded. "He died giving us a chance to escape. I carried his tags back. Eagle hasn't spoken of it since."

Jay walked along the wall of names. There it was: Harrier. Status: Disavowed.

"They erased him," Jay said bitterly.

"They tried," Cardinal murmured. "But we remember. We all remember."

Jay hesitated, then said, "I found a note in his old Bible. It read: 'To stand for what's right means sometimes standing alone. But never without purpose.'"

Cardinal bowed his head. "Then your father's still guiding you."

Jay let the silence settle. Then: "I'm not sure I believe. Not in what he did. Not in anything."

"That's alright," Cardinal said gently. "Belief isn't a uniform. It's a feather—you carry it or you don't. But it changes how you fly."

Jay nodded slowly and made his way out, talons echoing in the silence. The chapel door shut softly behind him.

Cardinal stood at the altar once more, eyes closed, beak bowed. His voice was scarcely more than a breath. "Guide him, Father," he whispered. "May his wings stay strong, and may the wind rise gently beneath them when the storm comes."

Chapter 6: Finch's Wire

Jay entered the tech bay to a blast of punk music roaring from somewhere deep within the cords and consoles. The air smelled of solder, hot circuitry, and the sharp metallic bite of ozone. Screens glowed everywhere. Walls, desks, suspended panes of light drifting through the air like constellations made of code.

Finch sat in the middle of the storm.

The small bird's wings stretched across two different keyboards, headset crooked sideways over one ear. His tail tapped rhythm against a coil of fiber cable while lines of code poured across half a dozen monitors. A soldering iron hissed beside a half-disassembled transmitter.

"Jaybird!" Finch chirped without looking up. "Welcome to the magic nest. We break things here. Usually with purpose. Sometimes… enthusiastically."

Jay blinked. "Do you always talk this fast?"

"Nope," Finch said, spinning his hovering perch around. "Just when I'm highly caffeinated."

He tossed Jay a small data stick.

“Which is, like, always.”

Jay caught it.

“Sit. Don’t touch the red buttons. Especially the blinking ones. Actually, just don’t touch anything.”

Jay folded his wings and looked around.

Banks of monitors displayed encrypted feeds, global network traffic, foreign language transmissions, and thousands of moving data points. Code cascaded like waterfalls across transparent screens.

In one corner, a monitor showed a baseball game. Sunlight spilled across a stadium field as brown-and-gold uniforms flashed across bright green turf.

Jay tilted his head toward the corner monitor. “You watch baseball in here?”

Finch glanced over and groaned. “Yeah.”

He tapped the screen. “And cry when we lose.”

Jay smiled. “That often?”

Finch sighed dramatically. “More often than I’d like.”

He leaned back in his hovering perch. “Loyalty’s a lifestyle. Born and raised San Diego. Been riding with the team since my mom pushed me from the nest.”

Jay studied the screen. Brown and yellow uniforms flashed across the field. “Interesting color choice.”

Finch narrowed his eyes. “Careful, Jaybird.” He puffed his chest slightly. “I look fantastic in yellow.”

Jay snorted.

Finch pointed at him. “And don’t think I haven’t noticed something suspicious about you.”

Jay raised an eyebrow. “Suspicious?”

“Blue feathers. Blue name. Blue attitude.” Finch leaned forward dramatically. “You’re not secretly a Toronto fan, are you?”

Jay straightened immediately. “I am not a traitor to this great nation.”

Finch burst out laughing. “Relax, patriot. I was just checking.”

Jay nodded toward the screen. “So you watch every game?”

“Every one I can,” Finch said. “Even when we’re down six runs in the ninth.”

Jay chuckled. “So what’s all this?”

Finch spun toward the central console. “This,” he said, spreading one wing toward the glowing displays, “is the digital front.”

The screens shifted instantly.

Network maps unfolded across the walls. Firewalls layered over global communication routes. Autonomous probes crawled through distant servers like mechanical insects.

“Where the real war happens.”

He tapped a display.

A coded stream pulsed across the screen in repeating fractal bursts.

“See this feed?”

Jay leaned closer. “That’s the Vultures?”

“Or at least their botnet,” Finch said. “Thousands of hijacked systems bouncing signals through each other like a swarm.”

Jay studied the pattern. “They’re communicating.”

“Fractal pings,” Finch said. “Recursive routing. Distributed command structure.”

He leaned back, tapping his beak thoughtfully.

“ARGUS is back.”

Jay frowned. “And?”

“And it’s smarter.”

Jay looked at the screen again. “How smart?”

Finch shrugged. “I’m trying to build a predictive model to track their signal behavior.”

He gestured toward the flowing code. “But it’s like boxing with ghosts.”

Jay pointed to another open file. “What’s that?”

Finch tapped a key. The screen expanded into a sealed archive. “Encrypted cache,” Finch said. “Source tagged to DARPA.”

Jay frowned. “The Vultures stole it?”

Finch gave a crooked smile. “That’s the story.”

He zoomed in on the metadata. “But here’s the weird part.” The archive unfolded into a perfectly organized directory tree. “No corruption. No damage. No messy break-in traces.”

Jay tilted his head. “That’s not normal.”

“Nope.”

Finch leaned closer to the screen. “It’s too clean.”

Jay felt the implication settle. “Like it wanted to be stolen.”

Finch snapped his claws. “Exactly.”

Jay studied the code. “A plant.”

"Yep." Finch leaned back in his perch. "They want us chasing this while they're doing something else."

He paused.

Then his voice dropped slightly. "But that's not the creepy part."

Jay looked at him.

Finch opened another hidden layer of the archive. Buried beneath the DARPA encryption was a fragment of older code. A tag.

Jay leaned forward. "Whose?"

Finch hesitated. Then said quietly: "Harrier's."

Jay froze. "That's impossible."

Finch shrugged uneasily. "It *looks* like his old identifier. The one he used back when he was flying ops before they scrubbed him from the system."

Jay's voice lowered. "He's dead."

"Disavowed. Dead. Deleted," Finch said. "Yeah. I know the official story."

He tapped the code fragment. "Could be nothing."

He leaned back again. "Could be bait."

Finch gave a thin smile. "Or maybe the old man's playing hide-and-seek in the cloud."

Jay said nothing. The thought lodged in his chest like a splinter. Finch must have noticed the look on his face, because his tone softened.

"You know what the worst part is, Jay?"

Jay looked up.

Finch's wings had gone still. "I lost my sister in a blackout three years ago."

Jay waited.

"Whole power grid collapsed during a heatwave," Finch continued quietly. "Hospitals overloaded. Backup systems failing one by one."

His voice tightened. "She was twelve."

Jay felt the room go silent.

"Heart condition," Finch said. "Nothing dramatic. Machines handled everything. Monitors. Pumps. Regulators."

He stared at the screen. "She was talking about starting middle school."

His claws tapped the console once.

"Then the grid went dark."

Finch swallowed. "And so did she."

Jay lowered his head.

"All I got afterward was a death certificate," Finch said, "and a system error log."

His voice was barely above a whisper.

"That's what rage looks like in my world."

He glanced toward Jay.

"A corrupted file where a heartbeat used to be."

Jay spoke quietly. "I'm sorry."

Finch nodded once. Then forced a half-smile.

"That's why I joined the Aviary."

Jay tilted his head.

"To make sure machines don't get to write the last word."

Finch turned back to the screens.

"Here's the thing about machines."

He tapped the DARPA cache.

"They don't care about truth."

He gestured to the code rivers flowing across the displays.

"They care about instructions."

"They'll repeat a lie perfectly if you tell them to."

"They'll erase a name cleanly if someone writes the routine."

He looked at Jay.

"And birds—busy, scared birds—believe whatever the output says."

Jay folded his wings. "So what do we do?"

Finch answered immediately. "We carry the truth."

Silence settled between them.

Then Finch's claws resumed flying across the keyboard.

"Anyway! Depression hour's over."

He tapped a key. A map of the Nest and surrounding airspace appeared. "I rigged this system to flag micro-transmissions within two hundred miles."

A blinking point appeared on the map. "Got a ping twenty minutes ago."

Jay leaned closer. "Vulture recon?"

"Maybe," Finch said. "But they're hiding it well."

He zoomed in. "Signal bouncing through atmospheric interference."

He shrugged. "Like a feather drifting in the wind."

"Did you report it?"

"Already flagged it to Owl," Finch said. "But she didn't appreciate my label."

Jay smirked. “What label?”

“Spooky Bird Number One.”

Jay laughed. “She rename it?”

“Hostile Echo.”

Jay nodded. “Very Owl.”

Finch grinned. “Extremely Owl.”

He tossed a small scanner into Jay’s talons. “Take this.”

Jay turned it over. “What is it?”

“Field scanner. Hooks into your HUD.”

The casing was scuffed, and a small brown-and-yellow baseball sticker clung stubbornly to one edge. “If you get close to another ARGUS Egg, it chirps.”

Jay raised an eyebrow. “That’s reassuring.”

“Very friendly chirp,” Finch said.

Jay slid the scanner into his harness.

Finch watched him for a moment.

“For a guy who’s all about strategy,” Finch said, “you sure get yourself into a lot of messes.”

Jay smirked. “I get out of them.”

“Yeah,” Finch said. “After breaking half the equipment and annoying the entire team.”

Jay raised an eyebrow. “I’m not the one who tried to reprogram the vending machine.”

Finch grinned. “That was an accident. The chips weren’t supposed to get stuck.”

Jay folded his wings. “A tragedy. The whole team mourned for ten minutes.”

Finch scoffed. “Don’t knock the snacks.”

Then he grew serious again.

“Listen.”

Jay stopped.

“Don’t let the files tell you who your father was.”

Finch tapped the console. “Machines don’t get the last word.” He looked Jay straight in the eye. “We do.”

Jay nodded.

Just then, a brief flicker crossed one of Finch’s side monitors.

Finch squinted. “Huh.”

“What?”

Finch leaned closer to the screen. “Just a weird packet echo inside the Vulture traffic.”

Jay waited.

Finch shrugged. “Probably nothing.”

But the code lingered for a moment longer before disappearing. For a split second, a tiny symbol flashed inside the signal stream.

A white dove.

Then the signal collapsed into static. Finch shook his head. “Ghost code.”

Jay stepped into the corridor, the tech bay noise fading behind him. The scanner thrummed softly against his ribs. He thought of Harrier’s tag buried deep in the code. Of a twelve-year-old girl reduced to a system error. Of a world where lies could be printed cleaner than truth.

He would learn to read the patterns.

He would learn to test what the machines said.

He would carry what was real.

Because if they could erase his father—
they could erase anyone.

Chapter 7: The Long View

The Nest was quiet after lights-out. Most recruits slept in their roosts, feathers tucked, dreams drifting somewhere between training drills and open sky.

Finch did not sleep.

Jay found him on the upper platform overlooking the canyon, visor off, tools spread around him in careful semicircles. A half-dismantled comm unit rested between his talons.

"You're going to break that," Jay said softly.

Finch didn't look up. "Already did."

Jay stepped beside him, talons scraping stone. Wind moved through the canyon in low currents. Below, the river caught starlight.

"You've got 0600 flight block," Jay said. "You need rest."

Finch smiled faintly. "Rest is for systems that aren't being hunted."

Jay leaned against the railing. "ARGUS isn't hunting you."

Finch finally looked up. “It’s hunting everything.”

Finch held out the comm unit. “Sit.”

Jay frowned. “Why?”

“Because you’re going to lead one day. Eagles already sees it,” Finch said simply. “And leaders should understand the tools that keep their teams alive.”

Jay sat.

Finch rotated the unit open, exposing a cluster of micro-filaments no wider than whiskers. “Signal routing layer,” Finch explained. “ARGUS tries to predict patterns. So we introduce noise.”

He adjusted one filament. “This loop injects variance into our flight signatures. Makes prediction messy.”

Jay watched carefully. “You think it can’t track us?”

“It can,” Finch replied. “But not perfectly.”

He paused. “And that gap? That’s where freedom lives.”

Jay studied him. “You talk about freedom like it’s fragile.”

“It is,” Finch said. The wind shifted. Finch’s tone changed. Not theatrical, just quieter. “My brother lives in Newark,” he said.

Jay blinked. “You’ve never mentioned him.”

“Because he’s not Aviary.”

Finch turned a small tool in his talon. “He’s a schoolteacher. History. Loves debates. Lets his students argue anything as long as they can back it up.”

Jay nodded slowly.

“Last year, the district piloted a behavioral forecasting program. Not ARGUS. But similar architecture.”

Jay felt the shift. “They flagged him.”

"For what?"

"Low compliance indicators. Too much unscripted discussion. Students searching controversial topics after class."

Jay's feathers lifted.

"They suspended him for 'environmental destabilization.'"

"That's absurd."

Finch's voice remained steady. "It was legal."

Silence stretched between them.

"They reinstated him later," Finch continued. "After review. But the damage was done. Parents were nervous. Administration cautious."

Jay stared out into the canyon. "He didn't break any rules."

"No," Finch said. "He made room for thinking."

The wind moved again. "That's when I started studying ARGUS more closely."

Jay folded his wings tighter. "I get it," he said. "But ARGUS also prevents violence. You've seen the projections. It's saved lives."

Finch didn't argue immediately.

"That's the seduction," he said at last.

Jay turned. "Seduction?"

"Safety feels moral," Finch said. "Especially when it works."

Jay's eyes drifted across the canyon wall. A weathered carving had been cut into the stone long ago. A white dove above an olive branch.

Finch followed his gaze. "Peace symbols always look gentle," he said. "That's why they're powerful."

He resumed adjusting the comm unit. “But if a system decides what thoughts are too disruptive, what arguments are too heated, what emotions are too risky…”

He glanced at Jay.

“…it doesn’t just stop violence. It stops people from becoming something new.”

Jay shook his head slightly.

“You’re assuming the worst-case scenario.”

“No,” Finch said gently. “I’m assuming trajectory.”

He tapped the exposed circuit.

“Prediction systems optimize. Always. If disorder correlates with speech, speech becomes the variable to suppress.”

Jay considered that.

“But what’s the alternative?” he asked. “Let chaos grow?”

Finch smiled faintly.

“You think people are chaos.”

“No,” Jay replied. “I think fear makes them reckless.”

“And I think fear makes them obedient,” Finch said.

The words hung there.

Jay exhaled slowly.

“So what do we do? Tear every system down?”

Finch shook his head.

“No. We build better constraints.”

He finished sealing the comm unit.

“We don’t fight technology. We fight overreach.”

Finch handed Jay the unit. “Hold it.”

Jay took it carefully.

“Feel that?” Finch asked.

“It’s warm.”

“Because it’s alive with signal.”

Finch leaned back on his talons.

“Leadership is like that. You’ll feel heat. Pressure. Data. Noise. Everyone telling you what’s safest.”

Jay stared at the canyon.

“You think I’m going to lead.”

“I know you are.”

“Eagle—”

“Won’t be there forever,” Finch said quietly.

Jay stiffened.

“Don’t.”

“I’m not predicting loss,” Finch said calmly. “I’m predicting succession.”

Jay almost laughed.

“You and your projections.”

Finch grinned.

“Difference is, I don’t lock doors.”

Jay grew serious again.

“If ARGUS predicts a riot that kills twenty people… and it can stop it before it starts…, should it?”

Finch did not answer immediately.

“That depends.”

“On what?”

“On whether it’s stopping violence,” Finch said carefully, “or stopping dissent.”

Jay looked at him sharply. “That’s a thin line.”

“Yes,” Finch agreed. “Which is why no machine should draw it alone.”

Jay’s gaze softened. “And you trust birds more?”

“I trust accountability more.” Finch stood, stretching his wings. “Machines optimize outcomes. Humans absorb consequences.”

He looked at Jay again. “That matters.”

A distant training beacon blinked red in the canyon. Jay turned the comm unit over in his talons. “If ARGUS keeps growing,” he asked quietly, “what happens?”

Finch didn’t hesitate. “It stops asking.”

“Asking what?”

“Whether it should.”

The wind picked up. Jay felt something unsettled in his chest. “You’re afraid of it,” he said.

Finch smiled gently. “No.” He clipped his visor back into place. “I’m afraid of how easy it is to agree with it.”

Jay stood. “You think I lean too cautious.”

“I think you lean protective,” Finch corrected. “That’s why you’ll be good.”

He stepped toward the stairwell. “But don’t confuse protection with prevention.”

Finch disappeared below the stairwell.

Jay remained at the railing.

The canyon breathed in slow currents of wind.

"Finch talks too much."

Jay turned.

Eagle stood a few steps back in the shadows, massive wings folded neatly against his sides.

Jay straightened slightly. "Sir. Didn't realize anyone else was up."

Eagle stepped beside him and looked out across the canyon. "Hard to sleep when the world is trying to predict your next move."

Jay almost smiled. "Were you listening?" he asked.

"Enough."

They stood quietly for a moment.

Finally, Jay spoke. "Finch thinks ARGUS will eventually try to control everything."

Eagle nodded once. "Prediction systems always want more certainty."

Jay folded his wings tighter.

"But if those systems can stop violence… shouldn't they?"

Eagle considered that. "Let me ask you something first," he said.

Jay waited.

"When the wind hits a bird in flight, what can it control?"

Jay frowned slightly. "Angle. Wing position. Balance."

"Correct," Eagle said. "Can it control the wind?"

"No."

Eagle nodded again.

“That idea is called Stoicism.”

Jay blinked. “Stoicism?”

“Old philosophy,” Eagle said. “Very simple rule.”

He tapped the stone railing. “Control what you can. Accept what you can't.”

Jay thought about that. “That sounds… obvious.”

“It is,” Eagle said. “That's why people forget it.”

Jay glanced back toward the canyon. “So how does that help against something like ARGUS?”

Eagle's voice stayed calm. “Fear comes from trying to control things outside your reach.” He gestured toward the sky. “Storms. Machines. Other people's choices.”

Jay nodded slowly.

“But discipline,” Eagle continued, “comes from mastering what *is* inside your reach. Your judgment. Your courage. Your actions.”

Jay looked down at his talons. “So Stoicism is just… staying calm?”

Eagle shook his head. “No.”

He turned slightly toward Jay. “It's staying clear.”

Jay considered that. “Clear enough to act.”

Eagle nodded once. “That's why leaders study it. Because panic spreads faster than fire.”

Jay let the words settle. “What if the right decision still leads to something bad?” he asked quietly.

Eagle didn't hesitate. “Then you still make it.”

Jay looked up.

Eagle's expression hadn't changed. "Stoicism doesn't promise good outcomes," Eagle said. "It promises you won't betray your principles trying to avoid them."

The canyon wind rose again. Jay felt something steady inside his chest. Eagle studied him for a moment. "When the noise gets loud," he said, "run the drill."

Jay touched the small SOAR plate on his wrist.

Stop.

Observe.

Assess.

Respond.

Eagle nodded once.

"That's Stoicism in the field."

Chapter 8: Owl's Eyes

The intel chamber wasn't just a room. It was a hive.

Servers hummed low and steady beneath the floor panels, a constant mechanical heartbeat that never stopped. Hidden speakers whispered the voices of the world: police scanners from three continents, financial tickers that fluttered like nervous wings, encrypted bursts that arrived like rain striking tin rooftops. Dozens of screens painted the curved walls in restless light, their glow reflecting across polished metal consoles and the dark curve of Owl's feathers until she looked less like a living bird and more like a spirit stitched together from code and shadow.

The air was cool—precision-cool—the exact temperature where processors stayed calm and minds stayed sharp. No warmth lingered here. No softness. Every detail had been tuned for clarity.

Jay paused at the threshold, letting the sound wash over him.

If Falcon's training hall was fire, this place was ice.

Precise. Surgical. Unforgiving.

At the center of the circular chamber, Owl perched on a suspended platform shaped like a branch. It looked organic at first glance, but closer inspection revealed fiber-optic veins threaded through its surface, pulsing faint blue light beneath her talons. Data flowed through it constantly, feeding the systems surrounding her like sap through a living tree.

A cup of black tea steamed beside her perch.

Next to it sat something strangely old-fashioned: a steel-nib pen and blotter. The nib gleamed faintly beneath the lights, its reflection dancing across a ring of tea stain on the paper. In a room filled with fiber and glass, the objects looked like relics dug up from another century.

"You're late," Owl said without turning, her eyes locked simultaneously on three different feeds.

"You're charming," Jay replied.

She didn't smile. She didn't even blink. Her enormous dark eyes tracked shifting lines of code while her voice remained flat and controlled.

"Timing matters," she said. "A fraction of a second decides whether an Egg detonates in a city block or is neutralized in open air."

Jay drifted farther into the chamber, his gaze sweeping across the constellation of displays.

"So you built all this?" he asked.

"I optimized it," Owl said. "The framework existed before I arrived." Her talons tapped once against the branch. "But I made it useful."

The room filled with a quiet pause. Only the hum of cooling fans and the occasional crackle of intercepted signals broke the silence.

Then Owl gestured toward a massive wall of cascading code. Lines poured downward like a frozen waterfall of symbols.

"ARGUS isn't just listening anymore," she said. "It's learning."

Jay stepped closer.

"Each failure becomes part of its reflexes. Each success becomes a rule. It doesn't repeat. It evolves."

She paused briefly. “At first it reacted.”

Her eyes flicked toward him. “Now it predicts.”

Jay frowned. “Predicts what?”

“Everything it can observe,” Owl said. Her wing swept across a console and a lattice of data appeared in midair, glowing pale blue.

“Movement. Speech patterns. Social behavior. Decision thresholds.”

She looked at him again. “Eventually it will know what a bird will do before the bird knows it.”

Jay studied the projection, watching the strands of probability twist through the air like roots beneath ice. “It was meant to surveil,” he said slowly. “Now it attacks?”

Owl shook her head. “It manipulates.”

She leaned slightly forward, eyes reflecting the hologram. “A hive mind with prediction for bones. It mimics behavior, injects subtle chaos, and lets the pattern collapse on its own.”

A new set of screens flashed open.

“A protest becomes a riot,” she said. “A rumor becomes a war. It doesn’t shove—it nudges.”

Jay’s feathers rustled uneasily.

“That’s not intelligence gathering.”

“No.”

Her gaze settled on him. “That’s control.”

For the first time she turned fully toward him. The light caught her eyes like obsidian glass.

“And it has been repurposed by predators who do not believe in balance or restraint.”

Her voice remained calm, but Jay sensed something tightly coiled beneath it.

“They feed it hatred. Fear. Distrust. Decay.”

A new feed appeared showing a corrupted network map.

“The Vultures do not want peace,” she said. Her eyes darkened slightly. “They want silence.”

A small pause. “On their terms.”

Jay folded his wings slightly. “And they believe that will work?”

“Some of them do.”

Owl studied the projection carefully.

“They believe if you remove enough chaos… enough argument… enough freedom…”

Her voice dropped just slightly.

“…what remains will finally be peace.”

Jay didn’t like the way the words sounded.

“How did you end up here?” he asked.

For the first time her feathers ruffled. “NSA,” she said.

Jay blinked. “You?”

“I traced an unauthorized algorithm buried inside a social media app.”

She tapped the pen lightly against the blotter as she spoke. “Bright colors. Friendly interface. Harmless branding.”

Her beak tightened slightly. “Underneath it: siphoned profiles. Dissent flags. Personality indexing routed to an offshore cloud.”

Jay felt a chill crawl up his spine. “You reported it.”

“Yes.”

"What happened?"

"They buried it," she said.

Her tone didn't change. "Then they tried to bury me."

Jay said nothing.

"Disavowed. Falsification charges. Investigations that appeared overnight." She looked past him, as if seeing a distant memory. "I spent eight months off-grid."

The pen tapped once more. "Cheap motels. Diner counters at two in the morning. Moving every few nights."

Her voice softened slightly. "Learning which rooftops were unlocked. Which buses did not have cameras."

Jay lowered his head. "I'm sorry."

"I'm not," Owl said calmly. "Clarity requires distance."

She lifted the pen and aligned it precisely with the edge of the blotter. "In the shadows I learned how to see the light without being blinded by it."

A small pause passed.

"Eagle found me before the hunt became lethal."

Jay exhaled slowly. "You still believe in the system?"

"I believe in the principles behind it." She gestured toward the screens. "But systems are not immune to infection."

Jay tilted his head. "You mean it was always broken?"

"No." She tapped a console. "It was vulnerable."

A hologram of Earth appeared above them, slowly rotating in the air. Pins began lighting across the continents like distant fireflies.

"The Vultures found the seam."

Her talon traced a faint arc across the globe. "They slid a needle into the soft tissue of our institutions."

A new layer of data appeared beneath the surface. "Now the toxin lives in the spaces between our laws… our ethics… our trust."

Jay stared at the map. "What am I looking at?"

"ARGUS's whisper map."

The pins pulsed faintly. "Each one is a behavioral shift."

Another set of indicators appeared beside them. "Fear up. Trust down."

She highlighted a cluster.

"Food lines that turn into shoves."

Another.

"Traffic delays that become street fights."

A third.

"A rumor that becomes a fire."

The globe zoomed toward South America.

"This began as a refinery strike," Owl said, pointing to Caracas. "Two days later: missing shipments."

The timeline advanced. "One week later: burning cars."

Jay shook his head. "No coup?"

"No invasion."

She folded her wings. "Just rot."

The globe rotated again.

Another pin glowed along the West Coast of the United States. San Diego.

Jay's chest tightened.

"Finch's home."

"Yes." Owl glanced toward him.

"Patterns always touch someone you know." Her voice softened slightly. "That is how ARGUS erodes resistance."

A small pause.

"Not just with numbers." Her eyes returned to the map. "With wounds."

Jay stared at the spinning globe. "It's everywhere."

Jay's feathers rustled uneasily. "How do you even begin to fight something like this?"

Owl didn't answer immediately. Instead she turned her enormous eye toward him. "You answer that."

She flicked the globe. Cities flashed past.

"Rome."

Another flick.

"Buenos Aires."

Another.

"New York."

She studied him.

"Different continents. Different sparks."

Jay scanned the displays. At first he saw only chaos. Then something shifted. Like catching a wind current mid-flight. "They're not random," he said.

Owl waited.

"They're stages."

He pointed to the map. “First you thin the trust.”

Another layer appeared.

“Then you erode stability.”

Another.

“Then you strike when no one believes in each other anymore.”

He looked back at her.

“It’s escalation.”

A flicker of approval crossed her expression.

“Good.”

She nodded once.

“You see it.”

Her voice sharpened slightly.

“Always ask what the pattern wants.”

Another beat.

“Always ask who benefits.”

Her gaze locked on his.

“That is how you survive, Jay.”

A slight pause.

“That is how you lead.”

The words settled heavily in his chest.

A chime sounded. Owl brought up a new heatmap of the surrounding mountain ridge. “Finch’s tracker worked,” she said. A faint signal pulsed. “Signature from twenty minutes ago.”

Jay stepped closer. “Vulture?”

"Consistent with cloaked flight technology." She zoomed the map. "Grid seven."

Jay frowned. "And the second Black Egg."

Owl nodded.

"They're embedding them like spores."

A pause.

"Waiting for the host to breathe."

Jay exhaled slowly.

"Why us?"

Her voice remained flat.

"Because symbols inspire."

She gestured toward the Nest's insignia displayed on a nearby screen.

"The Aviary is more story than squad." Her eyes narrowed. "They want to pluck us from the sky."

A quiet beat passed.

"So the world forgets what flight feels like."

Jay studied the predictive models sliding along the edges of the display. Probability arcs bent like gathering storm fronts.

"Can we beat something that rewrites itself?"

Owl's talons flexed against the perch. "Knowledge is a weapon."

Her eyes darkened slightly. "And I am not merely an observer." She leaned forward slightly. "My ancestors hunted under moonlight."

Her voice dropped almost to a whisper. "Talons silent as snow."

Jay held her gaze.

"Don't mistake precision for lack of blood."

She tapped a console. "When the time comes…"

Her eyes flashed. "I strike."

Another screen appeared.

His flight profile.

Reflex times.

Biometrics.

"You've improved since Falcon's test."

Jay nodded.

"She pushes hard."

"She must."

Owl folded her wings.

"Everyone here is forged in fire."

Her gaze lingered on him.

"No exceptions."

Jay stepped back. "Thanks for the insight."

He turned toward the exit. "I'll report to Eagle."

"Jay."

He paused.

Her eyes gleamed in the shifting light. "Instinct saves you in the moment." She tapped the console. "But critical thought saves you from the moments you never see coming."

Jay listened quietly.

"Doubt is natural," she said. "But do not let it blind you."

She gestured toward the swirling networks. “Think.”

Another beat.

“Question everything.”

The map flickered again.

“Connect the feathers into wings.”

Her voice softened slightly.

“That is how you rise above the storm.”

Jay nodded once.

The lesson settled deep in his bones.

Then he slipped quietly back into the corridor.

The chamber door slid shut behind him.

Owl turned back to her screens.

In the lower corner of the console, a silent alert pulsed.

ARGUS anomaly—New York sector.

The waveform looked wrong.

Irregular.

Organic.

Almost like a heartbeat scribbled in code.

She leaned closer.

It wasn’t a command signal.

It was a learning signal.

Owl narrowed her eyes.

“It’s spreading,” she whispered.

Her talon hovered over the console.

Then drifted instead toward the steel-nib pen.

She jotted a note in tight, immaculate script beside the fading tea ring on her blotter.

Almost inaudibly, she added:

“And I’m ready.”

Chapter 9: The Vulture's Council

The chamber lay buried inside a wartime radio bunker half-claimed by the Atlantic.

Its corridors were slick with tidal seep and the stink of rust, carved into a cliff along Galicia's Costa da Morte—the Coast of Death—where storms had smashed fleets against jagged rock for centuries. The bunker had once served as a listening post during a war most maps had forgotten. Now the sea was reclaiming it piece by piece.

Salt wind clawed through broken ventilation shafts. Moss crept along the concrete walls like a slow infection. Somewhere far below, waves hammered the cliff face in patient rhythm, grinding the stone grain by grain. The Atlantic never rushed. It simply endured until the rock gave way.

Inside the bunker, candlelight jittered across scavenged technology. War-salvaged monitors were lashed together with braided copper cables that hummed with stolen current. Black-market processors whined softly beneath cracked casings. Old radio antennas had been repurposed into signal relays, feeding the chamber with data siphoned from passing satellites, municipal networks, and the scattered infrastructure of the modern world.

It was crude.

But crude systems were harder to trace.

At the center of the bunker stood a long stone table carved with old burns and fresh cuts. Time had etched scars into its surface, and tonight those scars flickered beneath restless light.

Vulture stood at the head of it.

Around him perched six predators—birds stripped of uniforms, stripped of flags, stripped of countries. Exiles of their nations. Apostles of a darker creed that had grown in the fractures between governments.

For a long moment no one spoke. The Atlantic thundered faintly through the rock.

Then Vulture broke the silence. “You know why we’re here.”

His voice was low and ragged, a serrated whisper that slid through the chamber and settled into every shadow. “They let the world rot,” he continued slowly. “While we starved, they feasted on illusions.”

He spread his wings slightly, and candlelight stretched his silhouette across the bunker wall. Taloned shadows crawled along the stone like living things.

“Phase One taught them to doubt.”

A cracked monitor flickered to life.

The screen filled with footage of a city unraveling—sirens screaming through narrow streets, crowds surging like a breaking tide, police lines collapsing as panic spread faster than command.

“Whispers,” Vulture said softly.

Another clip rolled. Power grids collapsing across entire districts. Empty grocery shelves. Arguments in public squares turning suddenly violent.

“Outages. Rumors. Fear.”

He leaned forward slightly, resting his talons against the scarred stone.

“Empty shelves.”

The footage froze on a riot scene.

For a moment the only sound was the distant sea.

“Phase One taught us something far more valuable than chaos,” he said at last. His talon tapped the monitor once. “It taught us their reflex.”

The predators around the table watched in silence.

“That victory,” Vulture continued slowly, “was not glory.” A thin smile crept across his beak. “It was calibration.”

He began pacing along the table while the footage continued to play.

“We “We learned how much pressure a democracy can take before it begs for a choke collar.”

Another screen flared to life beside the first, spilling cascades of data across the bunker wall. Lines of code streamed downward in relentless columns while graphs pulsed with spikes of panic and reaction.

“We harvested terabytes of grief and panic,” Vulture continued, watching the numbers scroll. “Behavioral telemetry from millions of frightened citizens. Every reaction became a measurement. Every fear became a data point.”

He lifted a talon toward the glowing displays. “Which voices move the herd. Which screens multiply fear. Which officials reach for emergency powers first.”

His beak tilted slightly in contempt. “They chose order over liberty in eleven minutes.”

The chamber fell still as the footage replayed: crowds swelling, sirens wailing, command structures collapsing beneath waves of uncertainty. Vulture let the silence stretch, letting the images speak for him.

“They showed us their instinct,” he said at last.

He turned slowly toward the predators gathered around the table. “And now we own it.”

The footage shifted again. Brownouts rolled through entire districts. Rumors ignited across social media like sparks through dry grass. Neighbors turned on neighbors while cameras recorded everything.

“Phase One bought us something else,” Vulture continued, folding his wings neatly against his back. “Time.”

He gestured toward the flickering monitors.

“Supply routes rerouted. Budgets broken. Eyes turned inward while they argued on channels and stages about who to blame. And while they argued…”

A soft metallic chuckle escaped him.

“…we seeded footholds.”

Encrypted recruitment feeds flickered across the screens—hidden channels, encrypted networks, the quiet migration of the disillusioned.

“And the frightened came to us,” he said quietly. “They always do. To be made strong.”

His laugh rattled faintly through the bunker.

“Proof of concept. Proof of weakness. Proof that the world will wear our hand… if we call it safety.”

Widow leaned forward first.

She was sleek and angular, her rimmed eyes glinting beneath candlelight. Knife scars traced pale lines along her talons, souvenirs from places where rules had stopped applying long ago.

“How soon until the Eggs mature?”

Ash shifted beside her. Even among predators he looked massive, his feathers uneven and scorched from chemical burns no government had ever publicly acknowledged.

“The prototype in Moldova destabilized,” Ash said in a low rumble. “Vaporized the whole block.”

Vulture did not blink. “Perfect.”

Ash chuckled. “Fear needs examples,” Vulture said calmly.

Across the table, Cipher spoke. Where eyes should have been, faint optical implants glowed inside hollow sockets. The lenses adjusted constantly, recording everything in the chamber.

“ARGUS is self-replicating,” Cipher said. “Feed it enough behavior and it predicts five steps ahead. Eventually it predicts the decision before the decision is made.”

He tapped the stone once with a claw. “We will own the future of war.”

Another tap followed. “But starve it and the blade dulls.”

A screen beside him displayed modeling decay curves. “Models overfit. Prediction collapses. Panic without pattern becomes noise.”

Widow’s smile sharpened. “Then we won’t starve it.”

Cipher turned his head toward Vulture. “Behavioral telemetry alone would take years to refine the model.”

Vulture’s beak curved faintly. “Which is why we accelerated the process.”

He tapped another monitor. For a brief moment a blurred schematic appeared—an encrypted architecture diagram layered with predictive structures that pulsed like a living brain.

“The artifact recovered in Istanbul,” he said quietly, “has already begun to teach ARGUS how to think.”

The predators around the table leaned slightly closer.

Widow tilted her head. “And it works?”

Vulture’s voice softened with quiet satisfaction. “Before Istanbul, ARGUS reacted.”

A thin smile spread across his beak. “Now it anticipates.”

The schematic flickered away.

Ash gave a satisfied grunt. Widow leaned back slowly, absorbing the implication. "Then the world is already late."

Vulture opened a steel case. Pressurized seals sighed as the lid lifted. Six Black Eggs rested inside, their surfaces smooth and faintly luminous. Each one hummed with stored power, ARGUS nano-seed pulsing within their shells like slow breathing.

"This does not explode," Vulture said quietly. He lifted one carefully, turning it so the candlelight slid across its curved surface. "It listens. It mimics. It roots."

He rotated the Egg slowly for the others to see.

"It spreads like dust through the city's systems—Wi-Fi, scanners, cameras, even the air vents. It listens to voices and follows footsteps until it learns the patterns of the entire city."

The Egg hummed softly.

"But it is hungry."

The others leaned forward.

"Isolate it for seventy-two hours and the model degrades."

Vulture placed the Egg back in its cradle and closed the case halfway.

"But keep it fed…"

His eyes gleamed.

"…and it becomes a scalpel."

Cipher's claw stopped tapping.

"And the moral cost?"

Widow clicked her tongue. Ash laughed quietly.

Vulture reached into his cloak and withdrew a cracked military medal. The ribbon was frayed, its metal surface dulled by time.

“What is moral about a nation that forgets its warriors the moment they fall?” he asked softly. “What is sacred in a system that shames strength and rewards weakness?”

His talons tightened around the medal.

“They taught me to kneel for bread.”

His voice dropped to a whisper.

“Now I teach the world to kneel.”

Cipher inclined his head.

“Then let the cities burn.”

Around the table no one objected. They had all bled for flags that later denied their names—Widow’s family hunted by drones, Ash experimented on by the nation he once served, Cipher blinded by the laboratory he built.

Once they had fought for different countries. Now they served something else. Control.

Vulture slid one of the Eggs across the stone table toward Widow.

“Plant it in New York.”

Her eyes gleamed.

“Beneath the library.”

A map appeared on the monitor behind him, revealing a maze of tunnels beneath Manhattan. “The old coal tunnels and steam lines still honeycomb beneath the stacks,” Vulture said. “No cameras. No questions.”

His voice lowered.

“Let it learn.”

A pause.

“Let it whisper.”

Widow slipped the Egg into a shadowed sling.

"New York owes me a debt," she said softly. "I'll collect it in whispers."

Vulture turned toward Ash.

"You'll prepare the air."

Ash cracked his neck.

"Give me a subway tunnel and a week," he rumbled. "I'll turn the air into a weapon."

Cipher lifted his chin slightly. "I will see without eyes."

A pause.

"Through theirs."

A thin tension ran through the room—Widow's quiet disdain, Cipher's calm certainty, Ash's low amusement.

Vulture watched them all. And allowed it. Sharp edges made predators sharper.

Another monitor flickered on. A file opened across the screen.

JAY.

"One of them is already compromised," Vulture said softly.

Widow raised a brow. "How?"

"Give him trails to follow," Vulture replied. "Enough truth to wound. Enough lies to mislead."

He tapped the screen. "Route a payload through Harrier's retired call-sign. Spoof communications using his father's dead protocols. Let decoy funds brush Jay's name for a heartbeat."

His dry laugh echoed through the bunker. "He will choose truth over orders."

A slow smile spread across his beak. “And when he does… he will lead them in circles.”

Widow’s eyes gleamed. “And when they look for a traitor…” She leaned forward slightly. “…they will find their golden boy.”

“It buys us what matters,” Vulture said. “Time.”

He slowly spread his wings. “Phase Two begins.”

The words did not sound like a declaration. They sounded like a promise he was repeating.

“Chaos is temporary,” Vulture said quietly. “Order is inevitable.”

The monitors filled with predictive simulations. “ARGUS will fracture their alliances. The Eggs will anchor our silence across their skies.” He leaned across the table, voice lowering into a venomous whisper. “When the collapse begins, they will tear themselves apart trying to find who to blame.”

A long pause followed.

“They will not see the war.” His beak curved. “They will only see each other.”

The screens stitched together riots, blackouts, and sirens into a single symphony of panic. “They will beg for silence.”

His voice softened. “And we will grant it. On our terms.”

Far across the world, deep within the Nest, a faint harmonic ripple threaded through Midtown static.

Owl leaned closer to her console. Two precise taps isolated the signal.

13.7 Hz.

It nested inside the noise like a hidden heartbeat. Not a message.

A fingerprint.

rotating maps of the mountain perimeter. Owl stood at the primary console studying a flickering thermal display that tracked movement across the eastern ridge.

"Confirmed heat signature," she said without looking away from the projection. "Cloaked. Low altitude. Flight profile suggests it's not one of ours."

Eagle entered from the northern corridor a moment later, broad wings held close against his sides while the emergency lighting reflected across dull flak armor. The room shifted almost immediately around him. Voices quieted. Movements sharpened. Eagle never needed to raise his voice to take command because command settled naturally into place the moment he arrived.

"Scramble recon," he ordered. "Falcon and Jay airborne immediately. Finch, jam every signal east of the ridge."

Jay felt the hesitation before he could stop it.

The delay lasted less than a heartbeat, but inside his own mind it felt glaringly obvious. Some part of him had instinctively paused to examine Eagle's voice before responding to it. The realization hit him with immediate shame.

"Already on it," Finch called from the lower operations deck. His usual humor remained present, but it sounded thinner than normal now, stretched tightly over exhaustion and nerves. "Building a sub-harmonic interference bubble over the eastern ridge. We'll black out drone traffic, radio chatter, and thermal relays for a few miles."

Jay moved toward the launch corridor while trying unsuccessfully to force the hesitation out of his thoughts.

Before Vineyard Haven, obedience inside the Nest had been automatic. Eagle gave an order, and the Aviary moved without uncertainty because trust had never required conscious effort. ARGUS had changed that in a single mission. It had not merely copied Eagle's voice. It had reached into the instinctive relationship between command and response and poisoned it.

The realization followed Jay all the way into the launch bay.

Falcon stood near the edge of the platform while technicians secured tactical harnesses and checked flight equipment beneath the rotating warning lights. The veteran operative glanced toward Jay as he approached, her sharp eyes studying him carefully.

“You look tired,” she said.

“Didn’t sleep much.”

“Nobody did.”

The answer lingered between them because both understood the reason without needing to explain it.

Security protocols throughout the Nest had tightened overnight. Authentication systems now required double confirmation before routing signals into command channels. Owl had reassigned half the communications staff to manual verification work because Finch no longer trusted the automated filters he himself had built. Even the analysts moved differently now, checking data streams twice before reporting conclusions. The mountain still functioned, but the atmosphere inside it carried a quiet tension that had not existed before.

Falcon stepped closer to the open launch doors and studied the darkness beyond the ridge.

“You ever flown silent intercept?” she asked.

“No.”

“Good,” Falcon replied. “You won’t overthink it. Stay on my tail. No flares. No chatter. No showing off against the moonlight. Silent intercept only works when you stop trying to look impressive.”

The hangar doors separated with a deep hydraulic groan, and freezing mountain air rushed into the bay hard enough to rattle loose tools against the walls.

Falcon launched first.

Jay followed immediately behind her.

The cold struck him hard as they burst upward above the ridgeline into the open sky. Thin moonlight cut through layers of broken cloud while the wind carried the sharp scent of pine and snow from the mountains below. Ahead of them, Falcon angled downward into the darkness without activating any visible tracking systems.

Silent intercept required precision rather than aggression. Every wingbeat mattered. Every adjustment risked visibility. The two operatives flew almost entirely by instinct and terrain awareness while the Nest disappeared behind them beneath the clouds.

The eastern ridge unfolded below in steep ravines crossed by abandoned transmission lines and jagged rock formations. Wind currents twisted violently through the mountain gaps, forcing constant micro-adjustments to maintain altitude and direction.

“There,” Falcon said quietly over the whisper-comms.

Jay narrowed his eyes toward the cloud layer ahead. At first he saw nothing except drifting mist and shifting moonlight. Then the shape emerged gradually from the darkness as something slightly wrong against the natural movement of the sky.

The silhouette moved too smoothly.

“Visual confirmed,” Jay whispered. “Single Vulture. Pattern unknown.”

“Flank wide,” Falcon ordered. “I’ll pull attention.”

Jay banked upward into a climbing arc while Falcon dove hard beneath the cloud layer toward the target. The Vulture reacted instantly with a sharp sideways maneuver that looked unnaturally precise before releasing a burst of static-charged shrapnel into the air behind him.

The metallic fragments screamed through the darkness.

Jay twisted sharply as the shrapnel passed close enough to tear through the air around his wings. One fragment clipped his secondary joint, sending pain flashing through his shoulder before vanishing into the ravine below.

“Stop trying to be fast,” Falcon snapped over comms. “Fast gets you killed. Clean decisions matter more.”

Jay adjusted immediately while crosswinds tore through the canyon ahead. Transmission lines stretched below him in black webs waiting beneath the turbulence, and instead of fighting the shifting currents directly, he shifted his angle and allowed the wind to carry him sideways through the gap.

Owl’s old lessons surfaced automatically in his thoughts. Don’t overpower the pattern. Use it.

Ahead of him, the Vulture banked toward the eastern ridge while Falcon pursued from below, forcing the target into higher altitude where the clouds thinned beneath the moonlight.

Something about the enemy’s movement bothered Jay immediately. The wingbeats looked too even and too controlled to feel natural.

Then Eagle’s voice crackled through the comms.

“Bluejay Two, hold your angle. Wait for confirmation.”

Jay froze for half a second.

The hesitation was tiny. Falcon probably never even noticed it. But Jay felt it with crushing clarity because his first instinct had no longer been obedience. His first instinct had been verification.

The realization hit him harder than the pain in his shoulder.

“Jay,” Falcon snapped sharply. “Now.”

He moved instantly.

Jay rolled downward through the clouds while locking onto the Vulture’s trajectory. The sonic trigger aligned across his visor, and he fired.

The bolt struck the target directly across the chest.

The Vulture convulsed violently before spiraling downward toward the ravine below. Jay dove after him automatically, trying to confirm the kill before the darkness swallowed the body completely.

Then he saw the particles scattering behind the falling figure.

Black flakes drifted through the moonlight like ash carried by the wind. They dissolved instantly when they touched his wings.

"Did I hit him?" Jay asked while circling lower through the canyon.

Falcon remained above him, scanning the terrain carefully.

"No visible body," she answered. "No impact confirmation."

The black particles continued thinning into the night air.

"He wanted us watching him," Falcon said quietly.

Jay frowned. "Why?"

"Because recon wasn't the mission."

They circled the ravine for another minute before returning toward the Nest.

By the time they landed, the launch bay had already transformed into a containment zone. Technicians moved rapidly between tactical stations while overhead scanners swept the returning patrol route with rotating blue light grids. Owl stood near the center platform studying a suspended heatmap projection while Cardinal waited near the edge of the bay.

"You two alright?" Cardinal asked as Jay folded his wings painfully against his sides.

Jay nodded once. "Faster than I expected."

Falcon kept her eyes fixed on Owl's display. "He fought like he wanted to be seen."

Owl looked up immediately. "Because visibility was the point."

Jay stepped closer while technicians scanned the residue still clinging faintly to his damaged feathers.

“What does that mean?”

Owl expanded the projection across the room.

“It wasn’t recon,” she explained. “It was delivery.”

The map zoomed toward the eastern ridgeline outside the Nest perimeter where a glowing marker pulsed steadily beneath the terrain overlay.

“A second Black Egg,” Owl confirmed.

The atmosphere inside the bay shifted immediately. Jay could feel it happening around him as the realization settled across the room.

Cardinal stepped forward slightly. “Is it active?”

“Dormant,” Owl answered. “But not inert. It buried itself beneath one of our environmental blind spots.”

Finch’s voice crackled overhead through the tactical speakers.

“I’m running a belly-scan now, and that thing is already syncing micro-pings against ARGUS traffic patterns. It’s learning our system behavior.”

The word struck Jay harder than he expected.

Learning.

The same word from Vineyard Haven.

The same realization that ARGUS was no longer simply attacking the Aviary physically. It was studying them. Measuring reactions. Testing vulnerabilities. Mapping trust itself.

Eagle entered the launch bay moments later.

“Lock the skies,” he ordered. “No one enters or leaves without authorization.”

Again Jay felt the hesitation.

This time Eagle noticed it.

The commander's eyes shifted toward him briefly before returning to Owl's display, but the glance alone was enough to make shame burn through Jay's chest.

Owl continued studying the projection. "We can starve the Egg before it matures fully. We cut wireless traffic, radio bleed, public vector signals, anything it can absorb into the predictive model."

"There's more," Finch added from overhead. "The telemetry header carried antique encryption tags tied to Harrier's old call-sign."

Jay's chest tightened instantly.

"Could be spoofed," Finch added quickly. "Probably spoofed."

Probably.

The uncertainty hung heavily in the room because everyone now understood what ARGUS could imitate.

Falcon stepped beside Jay while Owl expanded another section of the projection.

"There's particulate residue in the air corridor," Owl explained. "We can follow the trail for approximately six hours before atmospheric loss destroys it."

Eagle nodded once. "Then we move now. Falcon, you take the shadow while the trail is still warm. Team One starves the Egg at first light."

Falcon's posture sharpened immediately. "Understood."

Owl frowned at another display panel. "One additional anomaly. The Egg keeps referencing stacks metadata, Dewey tags, and municipal Wi-Fi beacons."

Finch paused overhead.

"That's library language."

Eagle studied the projection for a moment before turning toward Jay and Finch.

“Tonight, 2300 hours. Bluejay Two deployment. Soft retrieval only. If the operation becomes visible, you abort immediately.”

Jay listened carefully to Eagle’s voice as the order settled across the launch bay.

And for the first time in his life, hearing Eagle speak no longer guaranteed certainty.

Chapter 12: After Hours at the Stacks

The city slept under a thin drizzle. Streetlights blinked at their predictable intervals across Civic Center Park, their light reflecting off the wet pavement. The gold dome of the Colorado State Capitol glowed faintly through the rain. Somewhere beyond the western edge of the city, the Rocky Mountains rose into the darkness, hidden behind clouds and darkness. Across the plaza, the Denver Public Library stood quiet and still.

“Ground says the alarm runs on a lazy cycle,” Finch whispered from the gutter, rain ticking off his helmet. “Ninety seconds blind, then thirty seconds where the system wakes up and gets suspicious.”

Jay checked his band and pressed the SOAR plate.

“Stop. Observe. Assess. Respond,” he murmured—four count in, four count out. His shoulders eased. “Clean, not loud.”

Finch grinned. “Music to my ears, Jaybird. Ready to save story time from a robot ghost?”

They slipped through the skylight on the blind cycle and dropped onto a second-floor balcony.

Below them the stacks rose in tidy aisles. The children's wing glowed softly—paper moons, beanbag planets, a blanket fort shaped like a nest. Somewhere deeper in the building a ventilation fan hummed.

Finch knelt beside the shelf and slipped a small puck-shaped device behind a library tag labeled **BATS**. A tiny green light blinked once, then faded.

"That's a hush beacon," Finch whispered. "It dampens nearby signals—cameras, microphones, motion sensors. Makes us look like background noise."

Jay glanced down at it. "Why does it smell like mint?"

"Because my lab exploded once," Finch said. "Long story. Now everything I build smells like toothpaste."

Jay shook his head, smiling despite the nerves. "You smell like a candy store every time you're about to break something important."

Finch tapped the side of his helmet. "Incorrect. I only smell like this when I'm about to **fix** something important."

Jay glanced at the shelf tag. "Bats?"

Finch shrugged. "Hairy birds."

Jay stared at him. "They're not birds."

Finch stood and brushed dust from his gloves. "Look, if it flies at night and screams at bugs, it's basically a bird."

He slid a palm scanner along the banister. It chirped—once, twice—then settled into a steady, unhappy tone.

"ARGUS seed is alive," he said quietly. "Buried near the server closet under Children's. They hid it where noise looks like noise—story hours, Wi-Fi traffic, printer chatter, kid giggles. Smart and gross."

Jay's feathers tightened. "We starve it. No diet, no growth."

"Copy." Finch flicked his gaze toward the security panel near the circulation desk. "Clock's running. Ninety seconds blind. We tango."

They moved aisle to aisle, landing soft, breathing softer. Jay tracked the cameras tucked into corners like patient eyes. Each sweep had a rhythm. Each rhythm had a gap.

"Stop. Observe. Assess. Respond," he repeated under his breath.

The cadence steadied his nerves.

"Hey, baseball update," Finch whispered as they crouched behind biography. "We lost. Again."

"We?" Jay said. "I'm not sure I ever joined your team."

"Friendship clause," Finch replied. "You get the pain and the jokes. Baseball heartbreak too. Don't test me."

Jay shook his head. "Fine. But if I have to care about baseball, you have to care about proper footwork."

"Joke's on you," Finch said. "I only have two settings: chaos and precision."

They reached a narrow service door marked **STAFF ONLY**.

Finch popped the latch with a tool halfway between a paperclip and a magic trick. The hallway beyond was colder, lined with storage boxes and staff posters.

READ BOLDLY. SHARE STORIES.

A corkboard held a crayon drawing of a blue jay flying over a skyline with the words "**FLY HIGH**" written in uneven letters.

Finch stopped.

"Hold up."

Jay turned. "What?"

Finch pointed at the drawing.

"That. That's why we're here. Truth isn't just data. It's kids who get to grow up believing the world is worth reading."

Jay swallowed. "Carry the truth," he said softly.

Finch bumped his band against Jay's.

"Carry the—"

"—truth," Jay finished.

They smirked.

Finch snapped a quick picture of the crayon stars and sent it to Jay's band. "*Open when the sky feels heavy*," he wrote.

"This is why they hate us—free shelves, open minds," Finch murmured. "That's a country you can't program."

They pushed on.

The server closet was a shoebox of warm air and tangled cables. Finch's scanner went from unhappy to furious.

"Bookworm-01," Finch whispered, peering behind the switch rack. "Not a full Black Egg—just a bookworm node. Smaller, quieter. It records, learns, nudges. Feeds everything it hears back into the larger ARGUS lattice."

A matte-black disk sat like a shadow behind the rack, hair-thin wires braided into the library's network spine. A faint pulse crawled across its surface, slow as a heartbeat.

"Clean, not loud," Jay said.

He handed Finch a folded Faraday cocoon.

A Faraday cocoon was standard Aviary kit. A silver mesh blanket woven with conductive threads. Wrap it over a device and signals can't get in or out. To the outside world, the tech goes silent.

Finch reached, then froze. "Wait. Don't step forward."

Jay halted instantly.

Finch swept a penlight across the tile. A thread-thin red line glowed across the threshold.

“IR trip,” Finch whispered. “They upgraded. Rude.”

He slid a mirror beneath the rack.

“Three trips. Pressure pad back left. Thermal bubble over the node. ARGUS got fancy.”

Jay breathed once.

“Stop. Observe. Assess. Respond.”

Observe: red lines, heat bubble, hidden pad.
Assess: the bubble spikes if they lean warm. The pad screams if weight shifts. The lines sing if they break.
Respond: change the shape of the room.

“Two hush beacons,” Jay said.

Finch lobbed them overhand.

Jay thumbed both on. The mint scent tingled in the air and the space shimmered faintly.

The thermal bubble softened.

Seconds won.

“Bluejay ready,” Finch said, rolling a coin-sized jammer between his fingers. “Three… two… one—go.”

He rolled the jammer across the tile.

Click.

The IR flickered.

The scanner’s whine dipped.

“Window,” Finch said.

Jay slid forward, weight in his hands, tail barely touching the floor. The cocoon unfurled like a silver curtain.

He dropped it clean over the disk.

The pulse dimmed to a whisper.

No diet. No growth.

“Package quiet,” Jay whispered—

The jammer sputtered. The IR flicked back early.

Finch didn’t hesitate. He yanked Jay’s harness and dragged him clear. The line tripped anyway. A tiny pop cracked in the air.

Finch hissed and dropped to one knee.

“Finch!” Jay caught him. “You okay?”

Finch shook his hand, forcing a grin. “Spicy handshake. I’m fine.”

The scorch said otherwise. Jay taped the wrist quickly. Tight enough to brace, loose enough to move.

“Truth,” Jay said.

The jokes paused.

“Truth? I’m scared,” Finch said quietly. “And I’m fine. Both can be true.”

They secured the cocoon to Jay’s harness.

Footsteps thumped above. Night guard.

Lights brightened slightly in the hallway.

Jay peeked. Perfect angle for a fast choke and silent catch.

His fingers flexed. Then he let go.

“Conscience isn’t drag,” he whispered. “It’s a rudder.”

He nodded right.

"Option C."

They slipped beneath the blanket fort in the children's wing as the guard's flashlight swept the room.

Gold star stickers dotted the underside of the fabric.

"My sister loved these," Finch whispered. "Said libraries felt like flying without leaving the floor."

Jay breathed four in, four out until his heart slowed.

"Fear's loud," Finch murmured. "Truth isn't."

The beam wandered away. Silence returned.

"San Diego's bullpen would blow this save," Finch whispered.

Jay flicked him with a feather. "You're insufferable."

"And alive."

They slipped back to the balcony and out through the skylight as drizzle thickened into rain.

"Now," Finch said.

They climbed onto the roof and pulled the glass closed. Rain slicked the roof. Finch's foot slipped and he pitched toward the edge. Jay snapped a hook and hauled him back. The yank lit a hot bruise in Jay's shoulder.

"Add 'spotter' to your résumé," Finch panted.

"Team sport," Jay said, masking the wince.

They dropped behind the ledge. Finch tore a strip of gum and handed half over.

"Mint."

Jay chewed, wincing. "Does all your gear smell like this?"

"Only the good stuff."

Jay tucked the cocoon deeper into his harness.

“You pulled me back,” he said quietly. “Truth: I wouldn’t have cleared in time.”

Finch met his eyes. “Truth: you’d have found another way. You’re stubborn like that.”

The drizzle softened. The eastern sky began to pale beyond the rooftops.

Below them a city bus groaned awake and a cleaning cart rattled across the plaza.

“Kids will walk in here this morning,” Finch said softly. “Pick up books without something whispering fear. That’s a good day.”

“Carry the—”

“—truth,” Finch finished.

They tapped bands.

A promise.

They rose carefully.

“Time to bounce,” Finch said. “I owe you breakfast that isn’t gum.”

Jay glanced once more at the blanket-fort stars before stepping onto the fire escape.

Behind them, the lights of the Denver Public Library flickered on one by one.

Owl would tag the captured node **BOOKWORM-01** before dawn and trace its whisper back to a larger Egg somewhere out on the grid.

For now the win was simple.

They hadn’t broken in.

They’d held the door open for tomorrow.

Chapter 13: Echoes in the Flame

Smoke clung to the flight deck like a ghost. Jay stood at the edge of the observation platform, eyes fixed on the dark ridge where the second Black Egg had been found. His wing ached from the intercept; his shoulder from the rooftop save. It wasn't pain that kept him awake.

It was the silence.

Overnight, Owl had logged **BOOKWORM-01**—the library node Bluejay Two cocooned—and its whisper trail pointed straight at a **civilian grid station in Sector Twelve**.

Jay steadied his breathing and made himself remember. Cardinal—faith under fire. Eagle—calm is a choice. Owl—see the pattern. Falcon—be clean. Finch—carry the truth. He recited them until the noise in his head thinned.

Falcon landed beside him, crisp even at rest. "Can't sleep?"

Jay shook his head. "Not after what we saw."

"They want us edgy," she said. "Reactive. That's how ARGUS wins."

“Do you ever feel it?” Jay asked. “That split second when instinct says run, but training says fight?”

Falcon’s eyes narrowed. “Every op. Every time. Fear’s just another wingbeat—push through it.”

The mission alarm cut across the deck.

Owl’s voice came over comms, cool and exact. “Intelligence confirmed. Black Egg in active pulse mode. Local interference at civilian grid station, Sector Twelve.”

Eagle’s voice followed, low and steady. “Scramble. Containment and intel extraction. Cardinal, Jay, Finch—flight one: perimeter and visuals. Falcon—flight two: prep retrieval.”

Finch hustled past, tossing a portable jammer. “Move it, featherheads! We’ve got a Vulture whispering sweet nothings to the power grid. Also—Sector Twelve feeds the county hospital. ICU’s on that substation. We cannot lose it.”

Jay felt his chest tighten. Finch never mentioned hospitals lightly.

They launched.

They flew EM-dark – electromagnetically silent. No strobes, comms throttled to a sub-harmonic whisper, too quiet for most sensors to detect. Faraday sleeves wrapped around their harness relays.

Discipline over spectacle, Jay reminded himself as the cold punched into his feathers. Be clean, not loud.

The winds howled as they crossed the divide, cutting tight into a V. Sector Twelve spread ahead in the gray smear of pre-dawn: rolling hills, a sprawling solar field, and the substation—transformers breathing with unnatural blue flicker.

“Grid distortion confirmed,” Owl said in his ear. “EM frequency rising 0.7 every thirty seconds. ARGUS is seeding.”

“Three tells,” she added. “Pulse is phase-locked to 60 Hz, distortion blooms after each transformer cycle, and there’s a new sideband at 13.7 Hz. It’s not just pulsing—it’s learning.”

They rode hot/cold shears rolling off the panels. Arcing pops crackled across bus bars. Jay flattened into a gust instead of fighting it. Don’t overpower the pattern—use it, Owl had taught him.

Cardinal flared, landing atop a lattice tower and digging in. “Jay—high perimeter sweep. Eyes on everything.”

“Roger.” Jay climbed and spiraled wide. From up high, the grid looked like a dying heart. Streetlights winked in Morse-like sequences. Cars rolled to a stop mid-road. The town below was waking to a nightmare.

Finch skimmed low, erratic and fast as a loose spark. “This place is humming like a busted amp. Getting weird feedback loops.”

“Translate?” Jay said.

“Means we’re about to have company,” Finch answered. “I’m picking a cloaked broadcast. Could be ARGUS talking to itself—or worse, someone talking back.”

Cardinal shifted along the tower. “Deploy jammer. Find that Egg.”

Jay swept the east quadrant and saw it: a matte-black orb pulsing gently, tucked behind a loose panel on a transformer core.

“Visual on the Egg,” Jay called. “East quadrant, nested in the transformer.”

“Copy,” Cardinal said. “Falcon inbound with containment.”

Jay dropped into the yard and landed soft. The Egg’s hum found a resonance in his chest—wrong, like it was mapping him from the inside out. Cardinal—faith under fire, he told himself, and pushed closer.

“Finch?”

“On you,” Finch said, slamming down beside him, talons unsnapping his kit. “I’m copying the stream. But this isn’t just a relay—it’s adaptive.

Hands off voice channels near the core. Don't feed it our patterns. We're the evidence, not the contamination."

Jay froze. "It's building a model of us."

Finch's feathers bristled. "Yeah, and drafting countermeasures."

His HUD flashed a timer: 71:32:18 … :17 … :16.

"Clock's running," Finch said. "Seventy-two hours of fresh data and this thing sharpens into a scalpel. Starve it before then and it turns to noise."

A shadow cut the yard.

"Contact!" Cardinal shouted from above.

Two dark figures raked the sky, red optics glowing. They dove with talons crackling.

Jay pushed up hard, rolling into the climb as a shock pulse stitched the air. A blue arc leapt from a breaker, turning the space between them to white glass. The nearest Vulture snapped a turn with clinical grace.

"Stop trying to be fast," Falcon's voice snapped over whisper-comms. "Be clean. Clean decisions beat fast mistakes."

Jay cut speed, forced his breathing even. The Vulture struck with a vicious jab—he didn't meet it head-on. He bled just enough altitude to slip the hit, then rode a cross-gust to pivot behind it.

"Nice," Finch muttered, even as his claws flew. "Keep him busy—I'm mid-grab."

The second Vulture knifed toward Finch. Falcon arrived like thunder, a bronze blur, and smashed it into the dirt with a surgical strike. Her battle cry cracked the air.

Jay tangled with the first attacker—lean, scarred beak, movements too smooth to be natural.

"You are data," it hissed. "You are noise."

"Good," Jay said. "Then hear this."

He fired. The sonic bolt hit center mass—clean. The shape convulsed and tumbled—and black snow shredded off in a glittering wake. Not blood. Not feathers. Cloak debris that hissed away on contact with his wingtips.

Decoy skin.

Below, Cardinal speared from the tower and pinned the Vulture in a diving grapple. The attacker shrieked, flared a blinding burst, and snapped free into the mist.

"Status?" Jay called, dropping to Finch.

Finch held up a chip. "Partial stream. Enough to give Owl a nervous breakdown. Also—flag on the control bus." He squinted at a sideband. "Old crypto header. Looks like Harrier's retired call-sign—again. Probably spoofed." He grimaced. "But it's deliberate."

Jay felt the hook set behind his sternum. Finch—carry the truth.

Falcon hit the yard hard, wings wide. She snapped open a collapsible Faraday cocoon and dropped it over the Egg. The mesh hummed as it swallowed the signal.

"No diet, no growth," she said. "We carry it quiet."

Eagle's voice came even over the channel. "Confirm. Contain. Continue. We don't win by guesses—we win by proof."

Owl's tone stayed cool. "Cardinal, Jay—air cover to the west. Falcon, secure the package. Finch, maintain the block. I'm mapping a second transmitter—possible relay near the service road."

Cardinal rose with a powerful beat, circling overhead. "On your shoulder, Jay."

Jay vaulted up beside him. The yard below flashed blue, then dimmed under the cocoon. Sirens wailed in the town. For a heartbeat he saw a hospital roof lit in the distance and thought of Finch's sister. This is why we fight, he told himself. This is why truth matters.

The surviving Vulture broke away into the tree line, leaving only a faint sparkle of artificial ash.

Owl came back on. “Trail residue detected in the exit corridor—same particulate as last night. We can follow for six hours before the signature decays.”

Eagle: “Copy. Team One exfil with the package. Team Two prepares to follow the shadow at first light.”

Falcon gathered the cocooned Egg with calm efficiency. “Package secure.”

Finch snapped his kit closed. “And I didn’t contaminate the sample. You’re welcome, future Owl.”

Jay dropped to the ground beside Cardinal as Falcon herded them toward the perimeter.

“You okay?” Cardinal asked, eyes steady.

Jay nodded. “No hesitation this time. I calculated early, chose clean.” He drew a breath. “Just… felt like conscience was tugging me both ways.”

“Conscience is not drag,” Cardinal said. “It’s your rudder. Keep it straight.”

They moved as one toward extraction. The cocoon thrummed dully; the substation’s flicker faded without its diet. Over comms, Eagle’s cadence set the pace: “Confirm. Contain. Continue.”

Back at the Nest, the deck swallowed their talons with a familiar scrape. Falcon handed the cocoon to a waiting tech team. Finch pressed the chip into Owl’s wing.

“Partial stream,” he said. “And an attitude.”

Owl slotted it, eyes tracking fast. “Catalog pings, RFID queries… and the ‘stacks’ obsession again. Our library breadcrumb wasn’t a one-off.”

“Because whispers live there,” Finch said softly.

Owl's eyes narrowed, the shape of a pattern taking form. "Some wars win without shouting."

Jay stood at the edge of the bay, listening to the cocoon hum, watching the ridge cut the dawn. He took inventory again: Cardinal—faith under fire. Eagle—calm is a choice. Owl—see the pattern. Falcon—be clean. Finch—carry the truth. He wasn't just reciting them now. He was using them.

Eagle's voice carried from behind. "First light split stands. One team to starve any other Eggs. One team to follow the shadow."

Falcon's beak edged into a grin. "Call the shadow mine."

Jay looked toward the dim horizon where the Vulture had vanished, a faint trail of black snow thinning in the wind. Last night had been a test. The quiet op had been a whisper.

This morning would be an answer.

Chapter 14: Falcon's Gauntlet 2.0

The sim chamber woke like a storm breaking—floor grids glowing, wall panels breathing heat, ceiling fans whispering crosswinds. Falcon stood in the center circle, visor down, wings at half-spread like a loaded spring.

On the glass behind her, the duty roster ticked by: **Pelican — payload quals 0600; Hummingbird — ISR sprint drills 0900; Crow — night infill check 2300**—names Jay didn't recognize.

"Sector Twelve gave me telemetry," she said without hello. "We test where you were good. We break where you were lucky."

Finch waved from the glassed-in booth, already wired into a stack of consoles. "Hi. Hello. I'm the luck detector. Also the snack provider if we survive."

Owl sat at a shadowed station, data rolling across her screens like rainfall. Cardinal waited in the doorway, quiet as a chapel.

Falcon flicked a talon to the far wall. A city unfolded: alleys, catwalks, cable nests, vent steam. Black snow drifted in the air—decoy ash like they'd seen on the ridge.

"This is Gauntlet Two," Falcon said. "Rules: no resets. No flair. You'll get three scenarios back-to-back: silent ingress, hostage filter, exfil under adaptive fire. Civilians in play. Your SOAR band stays live. If you ignore it, it logs it."

Jay rolled his shoulders. The ache from the substation still lived under the feathers, a dull bruise. He pressed the band and felt the click.

"Stop. Observe. Assess. Respond," he breathed. Four in, four out.

"Clean, not loud," Falcon reminded, then pointed up. "Wind shear is real. Finch dialed it all the way up."

"You're welcome," Finch said.

Falcon's hand chopped. "Go."

—

Scenario One: Silent Ingress

The alley exhaled heat. A camera blinked. Jay hugged shadow, counted sweeps, and moved on the dead beat. He cut under a spinning fan, let the gust slide him sideways instead of fighting it—Owl's lesson: use the pattern.

"Stop. Observe. Assess. Respond," he whispered. The cadence steadied his chest. He floated over a laser trip line by shifting weight into his hands, tail barely skimming the grate.

"SOAR compliance: green," Finch said in his ear, pleased. "Look at you being all professional."

Jay vaulted a final gap and perched on a catwalk above a glowing node.

"Clean," Falcon said. "No wasted motion."

—

Scenario Two: Hostage Filter

Floodlights howled on. Mannequin silhouettes stumbled into the corridor below—civilians mixed with decoy hostiles; some wore heat packs to fool the eye. An ARGUS drone slid out of a vent like a knife, armed with concussive rounds. The node Jay needed sat behind the crowd.

"Collateral threshold: zero," Owl said. "One mistake and it's a failure state."

Jay's heart lifted and then kicked. The drone pivoted. He could beat it with a fast snap shot. He *knew* he could.

"Stop," he told himself. The shot glittered in his mind like the easy answer.

He assessed. Wind vector, bystanders, bounce. He chose a banked sonic to curve around the crowd.

He fired.

The round kissed a hanging cable, shaved a fraction off its arc, and detonated against a decoy pack that read as "civilian."

Red washed the room.

"Failure state," Owl said, soft but final. "Collateral exceeded."

Jay's stomach fell straight through him. He'd been clean… until he wasn't.

Falcon didn't blink. "Scenario Three. You still have to get out."

—

Scenario Three: Exfil Under Adaptive Fire

The walls peeled and reformed into a rooftop field—vents, ducts, antennae. Three drones fanned wide and learned on the fly. Jay tried to outrun the math. Bad choice. He took a sting to the shoulder, then another to the thigh. Not maiming. Enough to shout.

"Stop trying to be fast," Falcon snapped. "Be clean."

Jay slammed the band. "Stop. Observe. Assess. Respond."

He bled speed, let a crosswind carry him under a duct, then used the suction off a spinning fan to sling him onto a better angle. Two drones overshot. He dropped a hush beacon, cut their ears for one breath, and slid off the roof's edge to vanish under the lip.

He made the line.

The chamber cooled. The city died.

Silence grabbed the room.

Falcon faced him. “Results: ingress clean. Exfil adapted. Hostage filter—fail. We don’t sugarcoat here.”

Jay kept his chin level. He could feel his pulse banging at his throat. “Copy.”

Finch’s voice was gentle. “For the record, the miss was by a hair. Cable sway. You read it; you just didn’t give it enough room.”

“That hair is the difference between a plaque and a funeral,” Falcon said. “We fix it now.”

Jay nodded, jaw tight. The failure burned. Part of him wanted to grab a reset. Part wanted to rip the visor off and hide.

Neither option was a choice.

He pressed the band again. Four in, four out. Calm is a choice, Eagle had said. He made it.

“Again?” Jay asked.

Falcon shook her head. “No sim reset. You don’t always get do-overs. But you *do* get a field drill.”

She pointed at the far exit. “Real-world gauntlet. Hush-route on the outer roof. Objective: recover a tagged data slug from Vent C-12 without tripping Owl’s decibel ceiling or Finch’s motion fence. Live wind. Wet metal. ‘Clean not loud’ or don’t bother.”

Finch brightened. “Owl set the meter to ‘angry librarian.’ You’ll know if you break it.”

Cardinal stepped forward, placed a steady wing on Jay’s shoulder, and bowed his head a fraction. “Eyes clear. Wings steady. May the wind rise gentle beneath your flight.”

Jay breathed once more and moved.

—

Roof Drill: Clean, Not Loud

Night had sharpened. The Nest's outer skin glistened. Rain slicked the catwalks; mountain wind pulled in serrated bursts. Owl's decibel meter hovered in the corner of Jay's HUD like a stern teacher.

He made himself small—no hero silhouette against the sky. He *stopped* at each corner, listened to the breathing of the building, *observed* fan cadence and ladder rattle, *assessed* the clean line over the loud line, and *responded* with motion that looked almost lazy.

Twice he nearly reached for speed. Twice he chose patience.

At Vent C-12 he found the tag tucked under a rusted lip. The wind shifted hard. The meter ticked amber. He froze, counted four in and four out, then waited for the gust to ease and lifted the slug clear with two quiet fingers.

He came back the long way, avoiding the tempting jump that would ping the rail.

He crossed the threshold and handed Falcon the tag.

Owl's meter blinked green. "Decibel ceiling never broke," she said, approving and precise. "Motion fence did not alert."

Finch thunked his head softly against the glass. "You were boring," he said, grinning. "That's a compliment."

Falcon took the slug, weighed it in her palm, then set it on the rail with a click. "Sim fail. Field pass," she said. "You felt the sting. You didn't let it steer. That's the lesson."

Jay exhaled. The burn in his chest was still there, but it wasn't running the show.

Falcon nodded once. "Gauntlet Two doesn't exist to crown you. It exists to keep you honest." She turned away, already resetting the room for the next bird who'd need it. "Debrief with Eagle at twenty-one hundred."

Cardinal fell in beside Jay as the doors hissed open. “Failure isn’t the end,” he said, voice warm as candlelight. “It’s a teacher that speaks plainly.”

Finch jogged up, bumped Jay’s shoulder. “And for the record? If that was you ‘failing,’ I’m buying stock.”

Jay cracked a small smile. The sting didn’t vanish, but it settled where it belonged—inside the lesson, not over it.

He touched the band.

“Stop. Observe. Assess. Respond,” he whispered, and felt the calm find him again.

—

2100 hours. Observation platform.

Wind slid cold across the open deck. Eagle stood where the sky met the stone, quiet as always.

“Come in, Jay,” he said without turning.

Jay stepped up beside him, ready to talk about storms—outside and in.

Chapter 15: Talons of the Inner Circle

They called this stretch of Galicia the Coast of Death for a reason—fog, reefs, a thousand wrecks. Beneath the cliffs, a wartime radio bunker, half-claimed by the Atlantic, hunched in the rock. Inside, salt-bitten cables and salvaged panels flickered to life as the Inner Circle waited for Vulture to speak.

Vulture stood at a stone table etched by a hundred old knives. For a moment he listened—not to the room, but to the small receiver perched beside the map. A soft pulse blinked once.

Only then did he speak.

Around him perched three shadows that made whole bases nervous.

“The signal has been given. Operation ShatterWing begins,” he rasped, voice steady as a drawn blade. “We don’t need their borders. We break their belief, and the rest falls silent.”

He turned first to the hulking figure whose feathers were singed at the tips, armor pitted and patched a dozen ways.

“Ash,” Vulture said. “You are the knock they never hear.”

Ash's beak crooked into something like a grin. "Then let's give them a door to remember."

Ash

Youngstown, Ohio, years ago

Ash grew up in a town built around a dead factory and a cracked dam. Sirens were lullabies. Rolling blackouts were the seasons. When the grid failed, Mill Road Medical Clinic—two rooms and a generator—failed with it. And when the clinic failed, people didn't come home. He learned early that darkness wasn't just night—it was danger.

One spring a storm hit hard. The dam groaned, the power died, and a family two streets over couldn't get their front door open after it warped in the flood. Ash pressed his palm to the wood, felt where it wanted to give, and popped it clean with one hard shove. After that, people called him when doors jammed, gates stuck, or someone was trapped. He wasn't loud. He was useful.

Soldiers rolled in with stamped promises: **BREACH & RESCUE**. They liked the way he could find a weak spot by touch. He trained fast—charge placement, hinge math, "two hits, one entry." His whole job was getting people out.

Then the mission changed.

The trucks showed up with lab crates and men in clean boots. The new orders were "testing." Gels that ate steel. Thermite charges that chewed through steel. They built door frames just to melt them. The rescue part faded. The breach stayed.

When the program was canceled, the briefcases left first. The reports said "successful evaluation." The town stayed dark.

Vulture found Ash standing in a crater that used to be a door on an abandoned training range. "They call this 'stability,'" Vulture said, voice like gravel. "All I see is a cage built from speeches."

Ash wasn't born a wrecking ball; he was made into one. The world had taught him which walls bend and which ones break. Once he learned chemistry could eat steel, he stopped asking permission. If a system kept the lights off and locked the doors, he would be the knock they never heard—and the hole they couldn't patch.

Kandahar Perimeter, 0200 hours

Dust breathed from a bunker wall. Ash pressed a palm to concrete and listened. "Hollow," he rumbled. "Cheap. Perfect."

Orange gel, neat rectangle. Timer—tick. The wall inhaled and vanished, a clean slice folding like cake. Sirens woke up late.

Ash moved like a storm that already knew the ending. A shoulder-check turned a desk to cover. A thermite tooth kissed a lock and it wept open. In the core, racks glowed like spine made of glass. He seated a matte-black Egg.

"Here's the whisper."

Lights stuttered. Outage rippled across the map—districts blind. Somewhere, a hospital generator coughed, then begged. A raider said, "We could hold this bunker."

"We don't hold," Ash said. "We break. When they rebuild, we break again. Fear remembers faster than walls can be built."

He touched his scorched beak to the Egg like a knight to a blade. "Hammerfall."

Widow

Test Range North, years ago

Widow flew her nation's best prototype—thin as a promise, sharp as a truth. Her squad trained by math: one precise cut beats ten loud punches. Then the program stalled. Parts embargoed. Meetings postponed. The team begged a committee for a landing-gear bolt. The committee sent a speech.

On a freezing night, her wingmate blew a tire on approach and slid off the runway, flames painting the snow. Widow climbed from her cockpit and screamed into the wind. A week later, a foreign panel called it "pilot error." Funding re-routed. Program canceled. The news moved on.

Vulture met her on a runway lit only by lightning. "You were not reckless," he said. "They were cheap."

Widow learned better math: cut clean, leave proof. Make liars blink.

Black Sea, dawn

Wind skimmed steel-blue water when the duel began.

A NATO interceptor patrolled a corridor it didn't know was lost.

"Turn south," Widow offered on open air, courteous as frost. "This lane belongs to silence today."

"Identify," the pilot snapped, popping a flare.

She smiled. "Widow."

He fired. She danced.

He had thrust; she had angles. Widow slid through his wake and plucked a sensor puck off his wingtip like a magician stealing a coin. Alarms screamed. He yanked left—hot, messy. She admired the fight and punished the noise: a ribbon-blade flick that tapped his stabilizer. Not to kill—just to teach.

"Brave," she said over the channel, "but noisy."

He clawed for altitude. She stitched a sleeping thorn to his fuselage—a tiny grapnel-splice—then let him limp home intact but humbled. His broadcast gear now carried a quiet extra thread that would answer when Cipher called.

She leveled and replayed a frozen frame of Falcon in Istanbul—the bronze blur cutting sky like a blade.

"Soon," she murmured, almost pleased. "A worthy partner for a dance."

Cipher

NATO Lab, years ago

Cipher once had eyes. He was the prodigy of “soldiers plus signal.” Budgets shrank. Corners cut. A test rig arced and burned. When he could see again through bandages, it was only in pain and sound. The investigation stamped “operator error.” Folders closed.

Vulture opened a door no one else would. “They buried your name to save their story,” he said. “Come write a louder one.”

Cipher learned to see like a radio—heat as color, breath as tempo, truth as lag in a voice. He didn’t hate sight. He preferred signal.

Undisclosed relay, 0300 hours

A room with no windows. Screens hung like lanterns. Cables draped over a pool of black glass. Cipher stood barefoot on the glass, eyeless sockets aglow.

“Profile subject: JAY,” he whispered.

The glass bloomed—flight arcs, micro-pauses, SOAR cadence, heart-rate climbs. Not video. An essence. He split it in two: Day-One Jay (raw, fast, loud) and Aviary Jay (clean after Falcon, calm after Eagle, anchored by Cardinal, patterned by Owl, sharpened by Finch).

The delta rang like a tuning fork. “Uncertainty,” he breathed. “My favorite instrument.”

On a side feed, a town library flickered in drizzle. Children’s wing. BATS shelf. Minted hush beacons. The ARGUS seed there died quietly—*starved.*

“Hello, Finch,” he murmured, almost fond. “You joke because you’re brave.”

Cipher built a voice from Jay's pulses—no words, just the *shape* of how he sounded when cornered. The room played back a line Jay hadn't said yet, only might: *I have to finish this.*

Perfect.

File saved: **MIRRORWORK—JAY—ALPHA**.

He braided threads—Eagle's steady cadence, Cardinal's prayers, Falcon's "clean, not loud," Owl's maps—and asked ARGUS the only question that mattered: *What breaks this flock fastest?*

The answer surfaced: Doubt.

He seeded three whispers: a clipped audio of Jay arguing with a ghost; a forged docket stamped with Jay's shadow; a security still that suggested a meeting that never happened. Not too neat. Not too big. Believable.

"Look in my mirror," Cipher told the dark. "Tell me which of you blinks first."

Back in the drowned bunker, waves pounded the doors like a giant's heartbeat. Vulture watched three feeds at once: a city stumbling in blackout (Ash), a pilot limping home humbled (Widow), and three little rumors traveling faster than truth (Cipher).

"They will call us cowards," he said. "They will say we cheat. Good. Let them shout. We prefer the quiet work."

He swept a wing across a map. Pins glowed on five continents. "Widow holds the lanes. Ash breaks the bones. Cipher eats the brain."

He tapped a smaller pin, set away from the others—Highland cliffs, a radio hush in old stone. "And if a certain legend stirs the air in Scotland, all the better. Ghosts have their uses."

Vulture's eyes hardened. "The United States is dangerous because it teaches—movies, music, open shelves, voices that argue and still stand together. The Aviary is that lesson with feathers. So we won't just beat them. We'll make them doubt. Break the story, and the heroes fall from the page."

Widow inclined her head, blade-slim and elegant. Ash rolled his shoulders like a door hinge testing its strength. Cipher tilted, listening to voices no one else could hear.

The storm hit the bunker doors and ran off in sheets. Inside, the plan breathed.

The Nest, 0505 hours

Owl's chamber hummed. New pins pricked the world: a sudden comms outage with a chemical signature (Ash), a NATO jet that came home talking to the wrong friends (Widow), and three artifacts that smelled like Jay but felt… off (Cipher).

Her eyes narrowed. "They're moving."

She flagged the map to Eagle, tagged the 13.7 Hz sideband to Falcon, and forwarded the "Jay" whispers to herself twice. On the rim of the screen, a children's library label flashed—BOOKWORM-01 contained. She allowed herself one small breath for Finch and Jay.

"Some wars win without shouting," she said, and reached for her next move.

Chapter 16: Signal at Walden

Walden appeared beneath them just after sunrise, tucked deep into a Colorado valley where the mountains crowded close enough to steal the morning light from the streets below. Snow rested along porch roofs and fence rails in smooth white bands, while thin streams of smoke curled upward from chimneys into the pale sky. From a distance, the town looked untouched by the tensions spreading across the rest of the country. The football field still carried faint traces of the previous night's yard lines beneath a dusting of snow, and the faded water tower overlooking Main Street still proudly declared HOME OF THE BLUE HAWKS despite years of peeling paint and hard winters.

Then the comms died again.

Static burst sharply across Jay's headset before collapsing into silence, and a warning band flickered across the lower edge of his visor as the system struggled to stabilize itself. Below them, the parking lot of Walden K-8 continued filling with trucks, minivans, and volunteer emergency vehicles while teachers guided children toward the gymnasium entrance in calm but hurried lines. Nobody was panicking yet, but Jay could feel the tension building from the air. People moved too quickly.

Conversations stopped halfway through sentences. Parents kept checking phones that no longer worked.

Ahead of him, Falcon adjusted her course slightly without losing altitude. "Single UAV above the valley," she said. "High and circling. It wants us looking at it."

Jay glanced toward the cloud cover but saw nothing beyond the glare of the rising sun breaking over the mountains. "Decoy?"

"Probably," Falcon answered. "Which means the real problem's already on the ground."

Owl's voice followed a moment later, calm and precise despite the interference still humming beneath the transmission. "The school backup network is carrying the same 13.7 sideband signal we encountered at the substation. Local communications are partially jammed, GPS routing is unstable, and the generators are cycling irregularly. Whatever embedded itself here is learning while it spreads."

Eagle entered the channel before anyone else responded. "Priorities remain unchanged. Civilians first. Secure the school. Restore communications. Contain the network intrusion before it expands beyond the valley."

"Copy," Cardinal said.

The team descended together through the cold morning air, dropping beneath the ridgeline until the smells of wet asphalt, snowmelt, and vehicle exhaust replaced the cleaner wind above the mountains. They landed softly on the gymnasium roof while Falcon remained airborne, circling high enough to monitor the valley without drawing attention to herself.

Inside, the school had already transformed into a temporary shelter. Folding cots lined the edges of the basketball court while volunteers stacked bottled water and blankets beside cafeteria carts pushed into the gym from the kitchen. Teachers moved from family to family with forced calm written across exhausted faces, trying to keep frightened children occupied with board games, coloring books, and paper cups of hot chocolate. Somewhere near the cafeteria entrance, somebody had started making pancakes on propane griddles, and the smell drifted warmly through the building despite the tension hanging over the room.

A handmade banner stretched across the far wall behind the bleachers.

WALDEN STRONG.

The paint was uneven, the handprints messy and overlapping, but nobody seemed concerned with perfection this morning.

A broad-shouldered hawk wearing a school administrator's jacket crossed the gym toward them with quick, efficient steps. Gray feathers ringed her eyes, though her posture remained steady despite the strain visible beneath it.

"Principal Swanson," she said. "Phones are down across the district. Bus drivers lost route contact nearly an hour ago. Half the parents can't reach their kids, and rumors are spreading faster than facts."

"We'll stabilize it," Cardinal assured her.

Swanson nodded once, clearly wanting to believe him even if exhaustion had started eroding her confidence. "The kindergarten class is sheltering in the library. Daycare kids are in the music room. We've got volunteer firefighters coordinating parking outside, but if communications stay down much longer..." She stopped herself before finishing the sentence.

Cardinal rested a wing gently against her shoulder. "We'll get your town talking again."

Some of the tension left her expression almost immediately, not because the situation had improved yet, but because someone else had finally stepped in to carry part of the weight with her.

Finch was already moving toward the interior corridors while diagnostic lights flickered across the compact equipment mounted against his harness. Two small drones unfolded from recessed compartments along his sides and skimmed low over the tile floor ahead of him like cautious insects.

"Signal's ugly," he muttered as Jay followed him deeper into the school. "Definitely ARGUS flavored."

The hallways still carried traces of normal life beneath the emergency. Children's artwork hung crookedly along bulletin boards. Trophy cases displayed decades of football teams, science fair winners, and veterans' assemblies. Construction paper snowflakes still clung to classroom doors from a winter decorating contest that suddenly felt impossibly distant from the crisis unfolding around them.

Jay found that more unsettling than the threat itself.

ARGUS no longer targeted military compounds or strategic infrastructure alone. It had learned to embed itself inside ordinary places where disruption carried emotional consequences instead of tactical ones. A frightened town could spread chaos much faster than a battlefield.

Finch stopped outside the server room and tilted his head toward the blinking racks inside. "There."

Jay followed his gaze and immediately spotted the matte-black disc hidden behind the network hardware. It was small enough to disappear among the cables and diagnostic lights, but the faint vibration radiating from it through the metal floor grating felt wrong in a way Jay couldn't fully explain.

"Parasitic learner node," Finch said quietly. "Not a full Egg. Smaller. Smarter. It piggybacks on existing systems and poisons everything connected to them while pretending to belong there."

"Can you isolate it?"

Finch looked mildly offended by the question. "Jaybird, isolating dangerous technology is basically my spiritual calling."

He carefully unfolded a Faraday cocoon around the device while streams of diagnostic data flashed across his visor. The change spread through the building almost immediately. Lights stopped flickering. Jay's comm feed cleared. Somewhere down the hallway, somebody shouted that the phones were working again.

Then came the shouting from the front entrance.

Jay turned immediately toward the noise.

Parents had begun crowding against the gymnasium doors as partial communications returned in uneven bursts across the district. Fear moved quickly through groups already exhausted by uncertainty, and the restoration of incomplete information had only accelerated the panic.

Cardinal reached the entrance before security or faculty could react. He didn't raise his voice or issue commands. He simply stepped into the center of the confusion with the same calm steadiness he carried everywhere else.

"Everyone's children are safe," he said, his voice carrying clearly through the noise without effort. "Transportation routes are being restored now, but we need space to move families safely and in order."

The crowd did not settle instantly, but it did begin to stabilize. People stopped pushing. Teachers regained control of the entrance lanes. Volunteers resumed directing traffic toward the registration tables. Watching Cardinal work, Jay realized that leadership inside the Aviary rarely looked the way he had expected before arriving at the Nest. The strongest people were not always the loudest ones.

Falcon's voice cut across comms a moment later. "Drone's descending."

Jay moved immediately toward the stadium roof access while cold air rushed against him the moment he emerged outside. Snow drifted across the empty bleachers below, and the water tower rose above the town against a sky that was finally beginning to clear.

He spotted the second node almost immediately beneath the home scoreboard junction box.

Smaller.
Quieter.
Waiting.

This time he worked quickly, securing the cocoon around the device while Falcon tracked the UAV circling high above the valley.

"It keeps exposing itself just enough to tempt pursuit," she said. "Whoever's flying it wants us distracted."

Jay studied the drone's movement pattern for another moment before shaking his head. "Too obvious."

"Exactly."

So they ignored it.

Below them, Walden slowly began breathing again as the school buses reestablished routes and the emergency dispatch systems stabilized. Teachers started organizing reunification lines while volunteer firefighters rolled portable grills into the parking lot and began cooking hamburgers for families who had been trapped inside the shelter since dawn. The crisis had not vanished, but the town had regained enough footing to begin helping itself again.

By late morning, the gymnasium had transformed from an emergency shelter into something closer to a community gathering place. Children laughed again. Exhausted parents sat together on the bleachers sharing coffee from cafeteria thermoses. Near center court, Principal Swanson stood beside the microphone preparing to announce the first round of restored bus routes.

Before speaking, she looked toward Cardinal.

He nodded once.

The entire gymnasium slowly rose together.

Teachers.
Parents.
Veterans.
Children.
Volunteers.

A hundred wings moved to a hundred chests as the pledge rolled unevenly through the room, followed by a crackling version of the national anthem played through an aging portable speaker. Half the crowd missed the notes. Nobody cared.

Jay stood near the rear entrance beside Finch while the sound filled the gym.

"My sister would've liked this place," Finch said quietly.

Jay looked across the room at the tired teachers, the firefighters serving food, and the parents finally beginning to relax now that their children were safe again.

"Yeah," he answered softly. "She would've."

When Blue Team finally lifted out of the valley an hour later, people lined the parking lot below waving as they climbed back into the clearing sky. A little kid near the football field saluted so enthusiastically he nearly lost his balance in the snowbank beside the road, and Finch laughed before saluting back.

Jay looked down one last time at the small town disappearing beneath them. The church steeples. The diner sign. The football field. The water tower.

Walden mattered because people lived there, and for the first time since Istanbul, Jay understood with complete clarity why the Aviary fought so hard to protect places most of the world would never notice at all.

Chapter 17: Operation Skybreak Begins

Operation Skybreak changed the rhythm of the Nest almost immediately. The corridors no longer carried the controlled calm Jay had grown used to over the past weeks. Technicians moved faster. Tactical displays updated continuously across suspended screens. Every launch platform remained occupied, every communications relay active. Even the sound of wings passing through the main corridors seemed sharper than before, as if the entire structure understood the stakes had shifted.

Jay stood beside Eagle at the central tactical table while the latest intelligence rotated slowly above the projection grid. Sector Fifteen occupied the center of the display: a military communications array built high along a ridgeline where three states shared emergency infrastructure routing. Satellite dishes and microwave towers clustered together like steel trees against the mountain terrain.

Owl adjusted the projection with a movement of her wing. “The array supports Emergency Alert routing across the region,” she explained. “If ARGUS gains persistent access to the network, it can manipulate public warning systems, transportation alerts, evacuation messaging, and emergency frequencies simultaneously.”

"In other words," Finch muttered from the edge of the room, "panic at scale."

Jay studied the map carefully. "Any civilian presence?"

"Minimal," Owl answered. "Night maintenance crews rotate through every six hours. Most systems are automated."

Eagle's attention shifted toward Jay then, steady and unreadable in the dim blue light of the operations chamber. "You've spent the last several missions learning how the team functions," he said. "Now you lead one."

The words landed heavier than Jay expected, not because he doubted the responsibility, but because Eagle rarely offered anything casually. Every assignment inside the Nest carried intention behind it.

"You'll take Finch and Cardinal into Sector Fifteen," Eagle continued. "Your objectives remain unchanged. Confirm the intrusion. Contain the network spread. Continue before ARGUS adapts to the disruption."

Jay nodded once. "Understood."

Cardinal stepped forward beside him, calm as always despite the growing tension inside the room. "We're ready."

Across the tactical table, Falcon lowered her visor after reviewing the array schematics one final time. "The terrain favors patience," she said. "Too much movement up there and the whole ridge lights up like a flare."

Jay understood what she meant immediately. The array did not need visible defenses to become dangerous. The towers themselves carried risk. Microwave horns. Transmission beams. Motion sensors. High-altitude wind shear. One mistake in the wrong location could expose the entire team before the mission even began.

"Keep it clean," Falcon added quietly. "The loud missions are the ones people remember because somebody failed."

Eagle leaned slightly closer to Jay, lowering his voice enough that only the immediate team could hear him. "The Vultures already know we're hunting the Eggs. Expect resistance."

Jay met his gaze steadily. “We won’t hesitate.”

“No,” Eagle said. “You won’t.”

Minutes later they launched into the gray edge of dawn.

The mountain air cut cold across Jay’s wings as the team moved low through the ridgeline valleys with no running lights and minimal comm traffic. Jay guided them beneath radar visibility wherever the terrain allowed, using the mountains themselves to break their signal profile apart while the eastern horizon slowly brightened beyond the peaks.

Sector Fifteen emerged gradually through the early light.

At first it looked almost natural against the ridgeline, the towers blending into the mountain silhouette until the details sharpened as they approached. Massive satellite dishes angled toward the upper atmosphere while horn antennas and transmission arrays rose from the rock in clustered layers of steel frameworks, suspended catwalks, and support cables. Red maintenance lights blinked dimly through the dawn haze.

Then the interference started.

Jay felt it first through his visor before Finch confirmed it over comms. Diagnostic windows flickered subtly along the edge of his display while static hissed beneath the communications channel.

“Signal contamination confirmed,” Finch said. “Definitely ARGUS flavored.”

Owl’s voice followed immediately. “The 13.7 sideband signal is synchronized directly to the array clock. It isn’t just embedded in the infrastructure anymore. It’s studying the transmission cadence.”

Jay slowed the team with a slight wing adjustment. “We stay dark from here forward. Cardinal, take the left high approach. Finch, stay with me until we clear the eastern dish cluster.”

The three of them descended carefully into the maze of steel supports beneath the main transmission array. Wind moved unevenly through the structures, carrying low mechanical vibrations along the catwalks and support beams until the entire facility seemed to pulse faintly beneath their talons.

Finch crouched beside a maintenance panel and swept a scanner across the nearby transmission lines. “Pulse activity’s ramping up,” he said quietly. “Aggressive pattern too. Whatever’s in here knows we’re close.”

“Find it before it adapts,” Jay answered.

The team separated.

Cardinal moved upward through the support structure with surprising silence for someone his size, disappearing into the upper catwalk shadows while Jay and Finch worked deeper into the transmission grid below. Around them, microwave horns hummed softly with invisible heat while relay dishes rotated in slow mechanical arcs above the ridge.

Jay noticed the movement a fraction of a second before the attack began.

A shadow detached itself from the upper framework and dropped silently through the steel lattice.

“Contact!”

Two Vultures descended almost simultaneously from opposite sides of the array, their dark armor absorbing the dawn light while red optics burned sharply against the gray metal structures around them.

Jay slipped sideways as the first strike scraped sparks across the catwalk railing beside him. The second attacker drove directly toward Cardinal, who met the impact head-on with enough force to rattle the surrounding framework.

The entire array erupted into motion.

Jay ducked beneath a support beam as another strike passed close enough for static discharge to crackle along his feathers. He used the momentum of the miss to cut sharply between two microwave transmission horns, feeling the heat shimmer around him as the updraft redirected his movement higher through the structure.

The Vulture followed immediately.

"ARGUS already lives inside your systems," the attacker hissed while twisting through the steel maze after him. "You're defending ghosts."

Jay ignored the words and focused on positioning instead. Fighting inside the array favored patience over aggression. Every beam, every support cable, every transmission surface altered airflow and movement angles unpredictably. One reckless attack would send both of them into the live transmission grid.

Below them, Cardinal slammed the second Vulture hard against a maintenance frame with enough force to bend steel supports inward.

"You fight well for a priest," the attacker growled.

Cardinal drove him backward again before answering. "Faith was never weakness."

Finch's voice cut sharply across comms. "Egg located. East antenna cluster."

Jay glanced toward the far side of the array and saw the countdown reflected faintly across Finch's visor as he worked beside an open maintenance cavity.

71:04:19

The same seventy-two-hour learning cycle they had encountered before.

"It's querying EAS infrastructure," Finch continued rapidly. "Emergency routing, broadcast frequencies, metadata archives…"

His voice hesitated briefly.

"And library stacks again."

Jay's attention sharpened immediately. "Same pattern?"

"Same obsession."

The Vulture attacking Jay lunged again, releasing a shock pulse that numbed Jay's left wing briefly as static raced through his harness systems. Instead of forcing the counterattack immediately, Jay bled altitude intentionally and rolled with the momentum until the attacker overshot the strike path.

Clean over fast.

Falcon's training settled into instinct now rather than conscious thought.

"Cardinal," Jay called, "lock down the east catwalk. Don't let them gain altitude. Finch, copy everything before containment."

"Already doing both," Finch answered.

Cardinal surged across the support framework and blocked the narrow catwalk access point with broad wings spread wide enough to fill the passage entirely. One Vulture checked momentum sharply while the second tried diving lower through the transmission supports, only for Jay to intercept him with a focused sonic pulse from his harness emitter.

The blast knocked the attacker sideways into a cable trough hard enough to scatter sparks across the catwalk below.

Meanwhile Finch worked furiously beside the open maintenance cavity while streams of data reflected across his visor. "The Egg's interfacing with literally everything," he muttered. "RFID systems. Microwave relays. Parking gate controls. This thing would probably interrogate a vending machine if you gave it enough time."

Jay reached him moments later and pulled a folded Faraday cocoon from his harness compartment.

"Almost there," Finch said. "Wait—"

His voice stopped suddenly.

Jay looked toward him.

"There's a signature buried in the control bus," Finch said quietly now. "Old header. Retired call sign."

Jay already knew what name was coming before Finch said it.

"Harrier."

The word settled heavily beneath the noise of the battle around them.

"Spoofed?" Jay asked evenly.

"Ninety-nine percent probability," Finch answered. "But deliberate."

Jay forced the reaction back down immediately. "Log it. Don't engage it."

Finch nodded and resumed copying the data stream while Jay unfolded the cocoon across the exposed cavity. The black mesh sealed around the Egg moments later, and the entire structure seemed to exhale as the pulse signal disappeared beneath the containment field.

The background interference faded almost instantly.

Transmission stability returned across the array.

"No signal," Jay said quietly while securing the final seal. "No growth."

Above them, the remaining Vultures disengaged almost simultaneously once containment locked into place. One launched into the high air beyond the ridge while the second vanished through the transmission towers toward the eastern valley before either Jay or Cardinal could pursue cleanly.

The facility settled back into silence except for the low mechanical hum of the relay systems stabilizing themselves again.

"Status?" Jay asked.

"Still breathing," Cardinal answered while rolling tension from one wing.

Finch checked the copied data stream and grinned despite the exhaustion written across his face. "I'd personally rate this mission somewhere between 'mildly traumatic' and 'professionally satisfying.'"

Jay laughed once despite himself.

Eagle's voice returned across the comm channel moments later. "Confirm."

"Confirmed," Jay answered.

"Contain."

"Contained."

A slight pause followed before Eagle delivered the final order.

"Continue."

The team launched from Sector Fifteen as the sunrise finally broke fully across the ridge. Golden light spread across the transmission dishes while emergency systems throughout the region quietly stabilized far below them. Somewhere beyond the mountains, hospitals regained uninterrupted signal routing. Emergency networks reconnected. Public systems resumed normal operation without most civilians ever realizing how close the disruption had come to spreading further.

That was the part Jay understood better now.

The Aviary rarely fought for glory.

Most of the time they fought so ordinary people would never know a war had almost reached them at all.

Back at the Nest, Owl met them immediately inside containment operations while technicians rolled the cocooned Egg toward isolation chambers deeper within the facility.

Finch transferred the recovered data stream into Owl's system. "Partial archive," he said. "EAS routing, infrastructure maps, and enough library metadata obsession to make me deeply uncomfortable."

Owl's eyes narrowed slightly while scanning the projection. "The stack queries correlate east again. Midtown routes. Tunnel access beneath the library system."

Jay looked toward Eagle as the larger operational map shifted above the room.

"The shadow's moving," he said.

Eagle nodded once. "Then we follow it."

For the first time since arriving at the Nest, Jay no longer felt like he was reacting blindly to the war unfolding around him. The patterns were beginning to connect now, not cleanly and not completely, but enough to reveal direction beneath the chaos.

Somewhere beneath the city, ARGUS was searching for something hidden in the stacks.

And now the Aviary finally had a trail worth following.

Chapter 18: Eagle's Lesson

The Nest had grown quieter as the night deepened, though the silence never fully settled anymore. Too many systems remained active. Too many teams were moving through the mountain at all hours now that Skybreak had begun. Even from the upper observation deck, Jay could feel the vibration of the base beneath his talons—the distant hum of generators, the low rhythm of transport rails moving equipment through the lower tunnels, the steady pulse of a place preparing itself for war.

The operations chamber below glowed in shades of blue and red. Every display in the room pointed toward the same target.

New York City.

The map stretched across the far wall in layered projections: Midtown streets, subway tunnels, utility corridors, maintenance shafts, forgotten infrastructure hidden beneath the island like veins beneath skin. Bryant Park pulsed faintly at the center of the overlay, and beneath it the outline of the New York Public Library glowed in pale gray beneath shifting tactical markers.

Near the corner of the projection, a timer continued its steady descent.

02:13:47

Jay stood at the entrance for a moment before speaking. Eagle remained near the open hangar overlook, watching the darkness beyond the mountains as if he could already see the mission unfolding somewhere far beyond the horizon.

“You wanted to see me?”

Eagle nodded once without turning. “Come here.”

Jay crossed the platform quietly. Far below the edge of the mountain, the eastern seaboard shimmered faintly through breaks in the cloud cover. Even from this distance, the cities seemed restless, their light spreading across the darkness in fractured gold lines that stretched toward the ocean.

For a while neither of them spoke.

The silence didn’t feel uncomfortable. Eagle never filled space simply to avoid quiet. That alone had taught Jay almost as much as any lesson inside the Nest.

Finally Eagle gestured toward the tactical display behind them.

“The cloak trail vanished under Midtown about an hour ago,” he said. “Owl tracked the residue as far as the library tunnels before the particulate decay accelerated.”

The image shifted slightly as Owl updated the projection from below. Underground pathways illuminated beneath Bryant Park and spread outward beneath the surrounding blocks in tangled layers of service corridors, maintenance routes, and abandoned transit access points.

“Signal activity’s increasing,” Owl said over the intercom. “The 13.7 sideband keeps surfacing beneath the archive levels. Whatever ARGUS is searching for down there, it’s getting more aggressive.”

Jay studied the map carefully. “You think the Vultures already found it?”

“If they had,” Eagle answered, “the signal would’ve moved.”

That made sense.

The countdown timer continued ticking steadily downward in the corner of the room.

Jay folded his wings slightly against the cold air drifting through the open hangar doors. “Today felt different.”

Eagle glanced toward him briefly. “How so?”

“I wasn’t reacting anymore.” Jay searched for the right words. “At Walden… at the array… it felt like I finally understood what everyone else already sees.”

“The pattern,” Eagle said quietly.

Jay nodded.

Outside, wind moved across the mountain face in long steady currents, carrying snow dust through the darkness beyond the platform.

“When I was younger,” Eagle said after a while, “I thought leadership meant never feeling fear. I believed calm was something certain birds were simply born with.”

Jay looked toward him. Eagle rarely spoke about himself unless the moment mattered.

“My first command went badly,” Eagle continued. “I froze trying to calculate every possible outcome before making a decision. By the time I moved, two birds under me were already dead.”

The words landed heavily, not because Eagle dramatized them, but because he didn’t.

“What changed?”

Eagle rested one talon lightly against the railing. “An old commander told me something afterward that I hated hearing at the time.” A faint trace of amusement touched his voice. “He said storms become dangerous when you stare at all of them at once. The trick is narrowing your focus until you can still move inside the chaos.”

Jay thought about that while looking back toward the map. Beneath the projection of Manhattan, dozens of potential routes now branched through the underground tunnels surrounding the library.

"Fear doesn't disappear," Eagle said. "You just learn not to hand it control."

Somewhere below the observation deck, Finch's voice suddenly burst across the intercom loud enough to echo through the chamber.

"I'm just saying, if we're going into ancient underground tunnels beneath New York City, somebody should appreciate how much extra gear I packed."

"You packed snacks again, didn't you?" Owl asked.

"Preparedness is leadership."

"That's not leadership."

"It absolutely is."

Jay laughed quietly despite the tension pressing through the room.

Eagle almost smiled.

The sound faded as the channel shifted back to operational traffic.

"You trust them?" Jay asked after a moment.

"With my life," Eagle answered immediately.

Not hesitation.
Not consideration.
Truth.

Jay looked back toward the city projection again while the realization settled more fully than before. Leadership inside the Aviary was never about controlling everything. It was about trusting the birds beside you when control became impossible.

Eagle stepped away from the railing and approached the tactical display. "Blue Team enters through the Bryant service tunnels. Cardinal takes point once you move underground. Finch handles containment and signal capture. Falcon's team remains topside for surveillance and intercept if the Vultures surface above street level."

Jay followed the routes across the projection automatically now, his mind already moving through the operation ahead of them.

"Priority stays the same," Eagle continued. "Protect civilians first. Capture the model if possible. Destroy what you must."

Jay nodded slowly. "If the Egg's active underground, open comms near the core could contaminate the data stream."

"Exactly."

"Then we stay dark as long as possible. Tight formation. Finch carries cocoon deployment. Cardinal watches tunnel approaches while I handle containment."

Eagle studied him quietly for a moment before nodding once.

"That's a leader speaking."

The words carried more weight than praise would have.

Jay glanced again toward the timer in the corner of the room.

02:08:14

"You ever stop doubting yourself before missions?" he asked.

Eagle looked back toward the darkness beyond the mountain. "No."

Jay waited.

"If the doubt disappears completely," Eagle said, "you stop respecting what the mission can cost."

That answer felt more honest than reassurance would have.

The operations doors slid open behind them and Falcon entered wearing full field armor, dark harness plates clipped tightly against her wings.

Snow dust still clung to the edges of her feathers from the exterior launch deck.

“Flight conditions are rough over the city,” she said. “Low cloud cover, crosswinds off the river, limited rooftop visibility.”

“Any sign of movement above ground?” Eagle asked.

“Nothing obvious.” Falcon adjusted one of the harness clasps against her shoulder. “Which usually means somebody’s hiding correctly.”

Cardinal appeared moments later behind her, calm as ever despite the growing pressure around the room. Finch followed carrying enough equipment to qualify as his own mobile supply depot, several compact signal jammers rattling loudly against the side of his harness while he walked.

“I would like the record to show,” Finch announced, “that tunnel missions are psychologically offensive.”

“You volunteered for this one,” Falcon reminded him.

“I volunteer for lots of bad decisions.”

Cardinal rested a wing briefly against Finch’s shoulder as he passed. “And somehow survive most of them.”

The room settled again after that, though the energy had changed now that the team stood together.

Eagle looked at each of them once before speaking.

“We are not going to New York to fight a battle in the streets,” he said. “We are going because something beneath that library is spreading quietly through systems most people will never even see. If ARGUS gains a stable foothold there, it won’t stay hidden for long.”

The city projection glowed softly behind him.

“Break the whisper before it becomes a voice.”

Nobody answered immediately.

They didn't need to.

Jay adjusted the strap along his harness and looked once more toward the map of Manhattan suspended above the operations floor. Somewhere beneath those streets, ARGUS was searching for something hidden deep within the stacks, and for the first time since Istanbul, Jay no longer felt like he was blindly chasing fragments through the dark.

Now they finally had a trail.

Falcon turned toward the launch corridor first. "Wheels up in two."

Cardinal moved beside Jay while Finch continued muttering complaints about tunnels, rats, ancient archives, and the statistical probability of underground disasters.

Jay paused briefly at the threshold and glanced back one final time.

Eagle still stood beside the observation rail overlooking the eastern sky, motionless against the glow of the tactical displays while the countdown timer continued falling behind him.

The storm was waiting beneath the city.

This time, they were flying toward it on purpose.

Chapter 19: Into the Stacks

Blue Team entered Manhattan from beneath it.

The service hatch hidden beneath Bryant Park opened slowly beneath a canopy of dormant winter grass and exposed irrigation lines, revealing a narrow maintenance shaft that dropped into darkness below the city. Above them, New York continued through its ordinary evening rhythms without noticing what moved beneath its streets. Sirens echoed somewhere far uptown. Subway trains rattled through unseen tunnels beneath the avenues. Steam drifted upward from street vents into the cold air while thousands of office lights burned across Midtown towers like distant stars suspended behind glass.

Below the park, the world changed.

The air grew cooler as Jay descended the ladder first, followed closely by Cardinal and Finch. The tunnels beneath Bryant Park felt older than the city moving overhead, as though they belonged to an earlier version of New York that had simply been buried and built over rather than erased. Steam pipes groaned softly overhead. Rusted freight rails disappeared into shadow. Condensation rolled slowly down ancient stone walls worn smooth by decades of heat and vibration.

Owl's voice remained low and steady through the comms. "Sideband signal is still active beneath the library district. RFID activity is spiking along the lower archive levels. The cloak trail hasn't fully decayed yet."

Jay adjusted the strap of the cocoon harness against his side. "Cardinal stays point. Finch keeps the containment package protected. No unnecessary chatter once we reach the stacks."

"Copy," Cardinal answered quietly.

Finch shifted the equipment rattling against his harness. "I'd just like the record to show that tunnels beneath one of the largest cities on Earth are objectively terrible places to spend an evening."

"You volunteered," Cardinal reminded him.

"I volunteer for many questionable life choices."

The tunnel curved gradually upward before ending at a vertical maintenance ladder bolted into the wall. Jay climbed carefully, feeling the distant vibration of the city pulsing faintly through the metal rungs beneath his talons. At the top, he pressed against the heavy grate above him.

The moment it opened, he stopped moving.

The Rose Main Reading Room opened before them with a scale Jay had not expected to find in the middle of Manhattan. Long rows of oak tables stretched beneath towering arched windows that overlooked Bryant Park and the glowing towers beyond, while green-shaded lamps cast warm pools of light across polished wood worn smooth by generations of readers. Far overhead, enormous chandeliers hung in the dimness like floating rings of gold.

But it was the ceiling that stopped him.

The vaulted canopy above the room had been painted as an open sky. Massive white clouds drifted across soft blue plaster so convincingly that, for a second, the room no longer felt enclosed at all. Evening light from the windows caught faint gold and rose colors inside the painted clouds, making them seem almost alive high above the reading room.

Jay knew it was paint.

Still, his wings shifted instinctively before he could stop them. Some part of him reacted to the open space overhead before his brain caught up, and for one brief second he wanted to launch upward into it.

Finch climbed through the grate behind him and froze as well. “Okay,” he whispered after several seconds. “That might actually be the most beautiful room I’ve ever seen.”

Cardinal emerged last, though even he slowed visibly beneath the painted vault overhead.

The library carried a silence different from the Nest. Not military silence. Not operational quiet. This felt older. Preserved. Like the room itself understood how many thoughts had passed beneath that painted sky over the years and had learned to protect them.

Jay lowered himself fully into the room and moved carefully between the long reading tables. Their wings remained tucked tightly against their bodies to avoid brushing the hanging chandeliers or the shaded lamps below. Even their footfalls felt intrusive here.

Owl’s voice returned softly through the comms. “Signal source remains beneath the reading room. Old conveyor and archive network.”

Jay nodded once toward the far side of the chamber. “Move.”

They crossed beneath the painted clouds in silence while the city glowed faintly through the great arched windows around them. Somewhere beyond the walls, traffic rolled endlessly through Midtown, but inside the reading room the noise arrived softened and distant, as though the library itself filtered the outside world into something quieter.

Cardinal slowed briefly near the center aisle and looked upward again. “Hard to imagine violence reaching a place like this.”

“Violence reaches libraries first,” Owl answered. “Always has.”

Jay found the service access door tucked discreetly along the western wall beneath a brass STAFF ONLY plaque darkened with age. Finch stepped forward without needing instruction and slipped a compact tool into the electronic latch. The lock clicked softly a moment later.

Beyond it waited darkness.

The lower stacks dropped beneath the library in narrow layers of steel shelving, freight lifts, maintenance walkways, and ancient conveyor systems built long before digital archives replaced paper catalogs. The temperature fell immediately as they descended. Dust drifted through their lights in slow motion while endless rows of metal shelves vanished into shadow on every side.

Jay felt the change in the atmosphere almost instantly.

The reading room above had felt sacred.

The stacks felt watched.

“Heads up,” Owl warned quietly. “ARGUS activity spikes whenever movement patterns stabilize.”

Cardinal stopped abruptly several yards ahead. A faint draft moved across the narrow walkway in front of him.

“There,” he said.

Jay narrowed his eyes. At first he saw nothing. Then the light shifted slightly against the aisle floor, revealing an almost invisible filament stretched across the passageway.

Finch crouched carefully beside it, scanner reflections flickering across his visor. “Not a tripwire,” he whispered. “Behavioral learning strand. It records movement patterns.”

Jay looked toward him. “Meaning?”

“It studies how we move through the space. Gait, rhythm, timing. Predictability.”

Cardinal examined the wire quietly. “Can we bypass it?”

Finch’s expression brightened slightly in the darkness. “Technically? Yes. Elegantly? Absolutely not.”

He demonstrated an uneven sequence of awkward half-steps and angled pivots across the aisle, carefully breaking any recognizable movement rhythm as he crossed the filament.

Jay stared at him. “You invented that just now.”

“I am an artist under pressure.”

Even Cardinal looked faintly skeptical before following him across.

Jay crossed last, forcing himself through the same ridiculous pattern while the invisible strand shimmered faintly beneath them.

Beyond the next aisle, Finch’s scanner pulsed sharply.

“There.”

The Black Egg rested behind a shelf endcap near an abandoned pneumatic tube junction, matte-black and faintly pulsing in the darkness beside a cluster of ancient conduit lines. Thin cables spread outward through the surrounding infrastructure like roots feeding through stone.

Jay felt the low vibration again the moment he approached it.

Not sound.

Attention.

The machine seemed aware of the room around it.

Finch immediately moved beside the Egg and began the copy sequence while streams of reflected code flickered across his visor. “It’s integrated into the building systems,” he murmured. “RFID tracking, ventilation timing, foot traffic patterns. It’s hiding its signal inside the movement of the library itself.”

Jay scanned the surrounding aisles while Finch worked.

Then he heard movement above them.

Not loud.

Careful.

Two shadows detached themselves from the upper shelves almost simultaneously.

Vultures.

Red optics ignited in the darkness.

One dropped directly toward Finch while the second drove toward Jay through the narrow aisle. Jay reacted instantly, ducking beneath the first strike while metal claws scraped sparks across the shelving beside him. The confined stacks changed the fight immediately. There was no room for wide aerial movement down here. No sweeping dives. No open sky.

Only precision.

Cardinal slammed into the first attacker hard enough to send an entire row of books crashing across the floor while Finch scrambled backward beside the Egg.

The second Vulture lunged again through the aisle.

“Your freedom is chaos,” it hissed.

Jay drove a short sonic burst into the narrow corridor before the attacker could complete the strike. The confined space amplified the impact violently, throwing the Vulture sideways into the shelving while black particulate scattered from the damaged cloak system like ash.

“Cloak residue confirmed,” Jay called.

Behind him, Finch triggered the snag net launcher. The compact mesh exploded outward through the aisle and wrapped around the second attacker mid-motion, crackling violently as the Vulture struggled against it.

“Temporary solution!” Finch shouted. “Very temporary!”

Cardinal solved the rest of the problem with one brutal strike that sent the trapped Vulture crashing through a rolling archive cart before both attackers finally retreated upward into the darkness above the shelves.

The stacks fell silent again except for drifting dust and the distant hum of the city overhead.

Finch exhaled shakily beside the Egg. “I officially hate library fights.”

Jay crouched beside him. “Status?”

“Copy complete.”

Together they lowered the Faraday cocoon over the Egg. The black mesh sealed around the device while the faint whispering vibration disappeared almost immediately beneath containment.

For the first time since entering the stacks, the room felt still again.

Then Jay noticed something protruding from the rusted edge of the old pneumatic junction beside the Egg.

A small metal canister.

Carefully wedged behind the conduit.

He pulled it free slowly.

Microfilm.

Old enough that the label had nearly faded away completely.

But not completely.

HARR-009

Jay stared at it without speaking while something heavy settled beneath his ribs.

Finch scanned the canister quietly beside him. “Could be a plant,” he said carefully. “Could also be real.”

Jay slid the film carefully into an evidence sleeve. “Either way, somebody wanted it found.”

Owl’s voice interrupted before the moment could settle further. “Microdrones incoming through the lower tunnels. Fast.”

Falcon cut across the comms immediately afterward. “Red Team’s deploying hush curtains over your extraction route. Move now.”

Blue Team retraced Finch's uneven movement pattern back across the learning filament before climbing rapidly toward the reading room above. Behind them, faint mechanical fluttering began spreading through the stacks like insects waking somewhere deep underground.

When they emerged once more beneath the painted ceiling of the Rose Reading Room, the silence overhead somehow felt even larger than before.

Outside the towering windows, Midtown glittered endlessly beyond Bryant Park while the marble lions of Patience and Fortitude stood watch over the library steps below.

Falcon's hush curtain shimmered faintly near the western exit, bending sound inward around the extraction route.

"Useful trick," Finch muttered.

Falcon glanced toward him while adjusting overwatch position near the roofline. "You're welcome."

Blue Team launched into the Manhattan night moments later, climbing above the library while the city unfolded beneath them in rivers of headlights, glowing towers, and endless motion stretching toward every horizon.

Jay looked once more toward the library below.

The stacks had returned to silence.

But somewhere beneath the city, hidden deeper within the systems ARGUS had already begun threading itself through, something had noticed the interruption.

And something had responded.

Chapter 20: Shadows of Doubt

Morning light filtered through the high slats of the Nest and spread across the operations floor in long bands of gold that cut across consoles, catwalks, and suspended tactical displays. Normally the base carried a steady rhythm at that hour. Technicians moved with quiet efficiency between stations, analysts traded updates across the operations pit, and maintenance crews rolled equipment through the lower corridors beneath the constant mechanical hum of the mountain. This morning, though, the rhythm felt uneven. Conversations lowered when Jay crossed the floor. A few heads turned toward him before quickly returning to their screens, and more than once he caught the unmistakable feeling that people had stopped talking entirely as he approached.

None of it was open hostility, but it was enough to tighten something in his chest.

From the mezzanine above, Eagle's voice carried calmly across the room before the silence could settle too deeply.

"For the record," he said, "nobody in this base flies under rumor or suspicion. We work with evidence. Nothing else."

The operations floor steadied almost immediately after that. Technicians returned to their stations, conversations resumed, and the tension loosened enough for the room to breathe again, though Jay could still feel traces of it lingering beneath the surface.

Falcon appeared beside him a moment later without any unnecessary urgency. “Briefing room.”

Jay followed her upstairs.

The doors sealed quietly behind them. Eagle stood near the tactical display while Owl worked through streams of telemetry projected across the central table. Cardinal waited near the far wall with his usual composed stillness, and Finch sat surrounded by datapads, wires, open diagnostic tools, and several snack wrappers that looked like they had already survived a long morning.

Nobody looked angry.

That somehow made Jay more uneasy.

Eagle motioned toward the table. “Sit.”

Jay lowered himself into the chair across from Owl. “What happened?”

Without answering immediately, Owl expanded several telemetry graphs across the wall display. Jay recognized the data almost instantly. Wingbeat timing. Recovery patterns. Turn tendencies. Tiny adjustments in movement measured down to fractions of a second.

“During analysis of the stacks operation,” Owl said, “we confirmed that ARGUS is modeling individual field behavior with much greater precision than we originally believed.”

Jay studied the projections more carefully. Some of the highlighted movement paths belonged unmistakably to him.

“My behavior specifically?”

“Yes,” Owl answered. “More extensively than the others.”

Finch leaned forward immediately, apparently worried Jay would interpret the statement the wrong way. “That’s not because you did something wrong,” he said quickly. “You’ve had direct exposure to multiple Eggs now, which means the system’s had more opportunities to study you. It’s collecting timing habits, movement preferences, reaction patterns, stress responses. Basically, you’ve become the most detailed behavioral profile in its dataset.”

Jay sat back slightly while the implications settled into place.

Cardinal spoke before the silence could deepen. “The important part is that nobody in this room believes you’re compromised.”

Eagle nodded once. “The Vultures want distrust inside the Aviary. The Harrier tags, the planted evidence, the timing of these discoveries — all of it points toward psychological pressure rather than direct infiltration.”

“They want isolation,” Jay said quietly.

“Exactly.”

Owl shifted the display again, bringing up the HARR-009 marker recovered from the stacks beneath the library. “The signature was inserted deliberately. ARGUS understands the emotional pressure points it’s creating.”

Falcon crossed her arms as she studied the telemetry. “Then we stop letting it dictate the pace of the game.”

Finch straightened immediately, interest replacing fatigue across his face. “Okay, now we’re talking.”

He spun one of the datapads around and rapidly expanded a rough simulation model across the screen.

“If ARGUS thinks it understands Jay’s operational patterns,” he said, “we feed it patterns we control instead. False telemetry. Fake movement signatures. Artificial hesitation points. We leak the model through the compromised relay Owl identified near the barge route and let the system build expectations around the wrong version of him.”

Owl considered the idea for several seconds before nodding slowly. "If ARGUS begins adapting itself around the false profile, we should be able to trace how it distributes and prioritizes the data."

Jay looked between them. "You can actually pull that off?"

Finch looked mildly offended by the question. "Jaybird, professionally misleading hostile artificial intelligence is one of my more marketable skills."

A small smile touched Falcon's expression before disappearing again.

For the first time that morning, the tension in the room eased.

Eagle stepped closer to the table. "Then that becomes the plan. We keep Jay off predictable flight patterns during the next operations while Finch and Owl build and leak the decoy model. If ARGUS commits to the false profile, we follow the leak backward."

Jay leaned back slightly, letting the idea settle in his mind. The situation still felt dangerous, but no longer shapeless. That mattered.

Owl slid a slate across the table toward him. The recovered microfilm image appeared on the screen beneath clean evidence markings and chain-of-custody tags.

"You should have access to the file," she said. "But not privately."

Jay nodded immediately. "Understood."

Without hesitation, he forwarded the file into the shared review archive where Eagle and Owl could continue tracking it alongside him.

Eagle noticed the gesture. "Good."

Finch bumped Jay lightly with one wing as he passed behind the chair. "And if your brain starts getting dramatic later, come find me. I'll annoy you back into emotional stability."

"That isn't how emotional stability works."

"You'd be surprised."

Even Cardinal laughed quietly at that.

The atmosphere in the room finally relaxed enough for everyone to breathe normally again.

Eagle straightened, and the shift in posture immediately pulled the room back toward business. "Finch builds the decoy model. Owl monitors the compromised routes. Falcon tracks topside movement around the relay chain. Blue Team stays on standby until we identify who's consuming the false telemetry."

Then he looked directly at Jay.

"You are not handling this alone."

The words settled more heavily than Jay expected.

A few minutes later the meeting dissolved and the operations floor resumed its normal rhythm around them. Mission boards updated with new routing paths while technicians redirected signal traffic toward the newly designated Ghost Pipe operation. Falcon paused briefly near the doorway before heading back toward the launch deck.

"Good work in the stacks," she said.

"Thanks."

Finch was already halfway down the corridor before turning around. "Baseball game after we trick the evil AI into humiliating itself."

"We're still going to lose."

"Probably," Finch admitted cheerfully. "But losing while eating stadium food is still a quality life experience."

Cardinal fell into step beside Jay as they crossed the mezzanine together. "Doubt visits everyone eventually," he said. "You just can't let it decide where you live."

Jay glanced toward him. The line worked because it sounded like Cardinal speaking naturally rather than reciting philosophy.

By the time night settled fully over the mountain, most of the hangar had gone dark.

Only a single maintenance light remained active near the far wall, casting long shadows across the deck while the rest of the chamber settled into low mechanical hums and distant ventilation noise. Cold wind drifted steadily through the partially open hangar doors, carrying the sharp scent of snow and stone from the mountains outside.

Jay climbed the upper catwalk alone and settled against one of the support beams overlooking the launch deck below.

For several minutes he simply sat there listening.

The Nest sounded different at night. Quieter. Less guarded.

He finally activated the slate on his wrist and brought up the image of the recovered microfilm.

HARR-009.

The faded label stared back at him through enlarged grain patterns and damaged edges that Owl's systems still hadn't fully restored.

The urge to leave hit him almost immediately.

Not recklessly.
Not emotionally.
Just persistently.

He could already picture the route east toward Manhattan, the cold air over the river, the endless lights stretching beneath the skyline. Somewhere inside that city there might actually be answers about Harrier waiting beneath layers of deception and planted evidence.

His thumb drifted toward the comm display.

A draft message to Falcon waited half-finished in the corner of the screen.

Need solo air. Ten minutes. Cover if possible.

Jay stared at the unsent message while the wind moved steadily through the hangar around him.

Below the catwalk, a night technician rolled equipment toward one of the maintenance bays while faint music echoed from somewhere deeper in the structure. The ordinary sounds grounded him more effectively than he wanted to admit.

ARGUS wanted him isolated.

That realization had become impossible to ignore now.

The behavioral modeling.
The Harrier breadcrumbs.
The pressure.
The doubt.

None of it worked unless it separated him from the rest of the team.

Jay leaned forward against the railing and looked back at the microfilm image again. Nothing new had appeared there. No hidden answer. No sudden revelation waiting inside the grainy still frame.

Just possibility.

And temptation.

Then laughter drifted upward faintly from below the catwalk. Finch again, probably still awake in the lab and talking too loudly for the middle of the night.

The sound pulled Jay back more effectively than discipline ever could.

This was his team now.

Messy.
Annoying.
Imperfect.
Real.

Slowly, he moved the message draft from Send to Save.

Then he locked the HARR-009 file back into shared review and shut the display off entirely.

The pull toward the city remained, and he suspected it would remain for a long time.

But not tonight.

And not alone.

He rose from the beam and headed back toward the stairs while the hangar settled once more into darkness, wind, and the steady breathing rhythm of the Nest around him.

Chapter 21: The Calm Before

Morning light spread slowly through the Nest, slipping through the high slats above the operations floor and turning the suspended tactical displays pale gold. The base was awake, though quieter than usual after the library mission. Engines idled low in the hangars beneath the mountain while technicians moved between consoles carrying datapads and cables with the tired focus of birds who had worked through most of the night.

Jay noticed the glances immediately.

They were brief. Subtle. Conversations lowered slightly when he approached, and more than once somebody looked away too quickly after recognizing him across the room. The mission beneath the library had been a success. They had captured another Egg, recovered the HARR-009 microfilm, and disrupted another ARGUS relay chain beneath Manhattan.

Still, something had shifted.

From the mezzanine above, Eagle's voice carried across the operations floor before the silence had time to settle too deeply.

“No one in this unit flies under suspicion,” he said calmly. “We work with evidence. Nothing else.”

The effect was immediate. The tension on the operations floor eased a little after that.

Jay kept moving.

Falcon appeared beside him near the central lift corridor, armored and already mission-ready. “Briefing room.”

He followed her upstairs.

The doors sealed behind them with a quiet hiss. Eagle stood near the tactical display while Owl sorted telemetry streams across the main console. Cardinal waited near the far wall with his usual calm patience, and Finch sat hunched over three separate datapads at once while absentmindedly eating something wrapped in silver foil.

Nobody looked hostile.

But everybody looked serious.

Eagle motioned toward the table. “Sit.”

Jay lowered himself into the chair opposite Owl. “What happened?”

Without answering immediately, Owl expanded a series of flight telemetry graphs across the wall display. Jay recognized the data almost instantly. Turn timing. Recovery angles. Wingbeat rhythms. Tiny movement habits tracked across multiple missions.

“ARGUS is adapting faster than we anticipated,” Owl said. “The system is no longer just observing combat encounters. It’s constructing behavioral models. Learning how we think and move.”

Jay studied the highlighted overlays. Most of them belonged to him.

“My profile.”

“Yes,” Owl answered. “The most complete one we’ve identified so far.”

Finch immediately leaned forward before Jay could misread the implication. “That’s not because you did anything wrong,” he said quickly. “You’ve just had more direct exposure than the rest of us. The Eggs have seen you operate repeatedly, which means ARGUS has enough material to start predicting tendencies instead of simply recording them.”

“It studies success,” Cardinal said quietly. “Patterns become useful once they repeat often enough.”

Jay leaned back slightly, letting the realization settle. “So the Harrier breadcrumbs weren’t just bait.”

“No,” Eagle answered. “They were pressure.”

The tactical display shifted again, bringing the HARR-009 microfilm tag onto the main screen.

“The Vultures want you isolated,” Eagle continued. “Distrust weakens units faster than direct attacks ever could. If ARGUS can predict how you move, it can eventually influence where you move next.”

Falcon crossed her arms beside the console. “Which means we stop giving it clean information.”

That immediately caught Finch’s attention. He spun one of his datapads around and brought up a partially completed simulation model already running across the screen.

“We feed the system a false profile,” he said. “A fake version of Jay’s operational behavior. Different recovery habits, different movement timing, different stress reactions. We leak the model slowly through the compromised relay Owl tracked near the river routes and let ARGUS build assumptions around the wrong pilot.”

Owl studied the proposal for several seconds before nodding once. “If the system commits resources to the false model, we’ll be able to track where the information spreads.”

Jay looked between them. “You can actually manipulate it that way?”

Finch looked mildly offended. “Jaybird, manipulating hostile algorithms is basically the only reason I passed engineering.”

A faint smile crossed Falcon’s face before disappearing again.

For the first time that morning, the tension in the room eased slightly.

Eagle stepped closer to the tactical display and expanded a new map over the wall. The East River appeared beneath layers of infrastructure overlays while a pulsing red marker blinked near several abandoned ferry slips.

“Our next target is here,” he said. “We believe the barge operating along this route is functioning as a mobile relay platform. Eggs are moving through the network using river traffic as cover.”

The projection rotated slowly while shipping routes, maintenance channels, and signal traces spread across the display.

“Blue Team handles infiltration and containment,” Eagle continued. “Falcon shadows topside with Red Team. Owl tracks the Ghost Jay telemetry leak remotely. I’ll coordinate reserve and extraction.”

Jay studied the barge layout carefully. Cargo containers crowded most of the deck while power systems clustered near the rear communications spine.

“Priorities?” he asked.

“Lives first,” Eagle answered. “Evidence second. Enemy third.”

Jay nodded once.

Finch slid a compact equipment case across the table toward him. “Two Faraday cocoons, one snag net, three hush beacons, and before you ask, yes, the beacons still smell like mint.”

“Why do they smell like mint?”

Finch hesitated. “You know, I respect you too much to lie badly this early in the morning.”

Even Eagle almost smiled at that.

Cardinal stepped beside Jay as the briefing began wrapping up. “Blessing before launch?”

Jay nodded immediately. “Yeah.”

Owl brought the HARR-009 still back onto the side display. “You’ll have access to the recovered file during the mission,” she said. “But keep it inside shared review.”

“Understood.”

Jay forwarded the file directly into Eagle’s linked queue without hesitation.

Not hidden.
Not private.
Shared.

Eagle noticed.

“Good,” he said simply.

The briefing dissolved a few minutes later as teams moved toward the staging levels beneath the hangars. Falcon adjusted the straps along her harness while Finch continued talking through signal contamination theories fast enough that even Owl eventually muted his channel remotely for several seconds.

“You muted me again!”

“Temporarily,” Owl answered calmly.

“This is oppression.”

“It’s volume control.”

By the time Blue Team reached the staging bay, the Nest had fully shifted into operational rhythm. Maintenance crews checked harness locks beneath bright overhead lights while technicians rolled equipment carts between launch rails. Falcon’s hush curtain rig rested along the far wall folded into a compact silvered bundle that looked too delicate to be military hardware.

Eagle entered the bay a moment later and the entire room instinctively straightened around him.

“Rules of engagement remain unchanged,” he said. “Minimal visibility. Minimal noise. We secure the relay, recover the data stream, and leave before ARGUS understands what happened.”

Jay nodded while securing the cocoon harness against his side.

Cardinal rested a wing briefly against Jay’s shoulder and lowered his head. “May your eyes stay clear and your wings stay steady.”

“Amen,” Finch added automatically before looking around. “Also hopefully no explosions.”

Owl’s voice arrived across the bay speakers before anybody could answer. “The relay is active. Sideband traffic at 13.7 hertz confirms network synchronization. The same archive metadata from the library stacks is present inside the transmission flow.”

“Then the trail’s still alive,” Falcon said quietly.

Minutes later Blue Team descended through the lower tunnel access toward the river channels beneath the city.

The air smelled of wet iron, saltwater, and old concrete as they moved through the maintenance corridors below the docks. Jay felt the pull toward the HARR-009 file again somewhere in the back of his mind, but it no longer carried the same sharp urgency it had the night before.

Not because the questions had disappeared.

Because he no longer felt alone with them.

By the time they reached the river mouth, the barge had already drifted into position against the current. Gray water slapped softly against its hull while stacked cargo containers rose above the deck in uneven rows beneath hanging tarps. Near the rear of the vessel, a folded crane arm rested motionless against the overcast sky like some enormous sleeping insect.

"Red Team in position," Falcon whispered over comms from somewhere high above the docks. "You've got clear air."

"Ghost Jay telemetry seeded," Finch added. "If ARGUS takes the bait, Owl should see where the signal spreads."

"First trace already tagged," Owl confirmed.

Cardinal pointed toward the port-side gangway where two guards stood near the loading entrance. "Quiet and deliberate."

Jay nodded.

They moved together across the gangway with practiced precision. Cardinal reached the first guard before the bird could react fully, controlling the takedown with enough force to end the struggle immediately without unnecessary damage. Jay intercepted the second before the alarm switch could be reached, redirecting the movement and lowering him silently against the deck.

The river remained louder than the fight.

Blue Team slipped beneath one of the tarps and into the interior cargo corridor beyond.

Battery arrays lined the walls beside thick communication cables that fed deeper into the vessel's systems. At the center of the compartment, the Egg rested inside a reinforced cradle connected directly into the barge's relay spine through thick braided conduits.

The matte-black surface pulsed faintly in the darkness.

"Definitely active," Finch murmured while unpacking the cocoon rig.

Jay studied the compartment carefully while Owl monitored signal traffic remotely through the comms. The Egg felt different from the others somehow. Hungrier. The vibration inside the room felt uneven, almost impatient, like the machine wanted something.

"Telemetry spike," Owl warned quietly. "The relay's reacting to the Ghost Jay feed."

“Good,” Eagle answered somewhere deeper on the command channel. “Keep it drinking.”

Jay steadied his breathing and let the room narrow into practical details. Mesh spacing. Cable routing. Distance to the relay spine. Cardinal holding the corridor behind him while Finch prepared containment beside the cradle.

Then he stepped forward.

Together, he and Finch lowered the Faraday cocoon over the Egg while Cardinal secured the relay cables feeding into the network core. The black mesh sealed around the device moments later, and almost immediately the pulse inside the compartment weakened into silence.

The surrounding hum of the barge softened with it.

“Signal collapse confirmed,” Owl reported. “ARGUS committed to the false telemetry stream. We’ve got movement across three linked relay routes already.”

Finch grinned while copying the data stream. “It actually bought Ghost Jay.”

“Don’t celebrate yet,” Falcon warned from above. “Two fast movers approaching the docks from the east.”

Jay tightened the final cocoon seal and looked toward the cargo hatch.

“Then we leave before they arrive.”

Blue Team moved quickly but without panic as they retraced their route back across the deck. Above them, Falcon’s team remained hidden along the surrounding rooftops while the river carried cold wind through the shipping lanes beneath the gray afternoon sky.

As Jay crossed the gangway, he realized something had changed inside him during the operation.

The pull toward Harrier remained.
The questions remained.
The doubt still existed somewhere underneath all of it.

But the mission had come first anyway.

And for now, that was enough.

Chapter 22: The Storm Breaks

Jay had not really slept.

By the time he stepped onto the operations floor, the Nest already carried the strained atmosphere of birds preparing for something irreversible. Tactical projections glowed across the walls in overlapping layers of maps, signal routes, thermal imaging, and relay traffic while technicians moved quickly between consoles without wasting words. The usual rhythm of the command floor had changed over the past several weeks. Conversations were shorter now. Jokes came less often. Even the sound of equipment seemed sharper inside the mountain.

At the center of the room, Eagle stood beside the primary display with his wings folded tightly against his sides.

"This is it," he said.

The room settled immediately around his voice.

"Owl traced last night's relay traffic to a forward Vulture position along the river. We believe it functions as a coordination hub for several nearby ARGUS networks. If we hit it cleanly, we disrupt their communications and expose part of the larger structure underneath."

The projection shifted, revealing a sprawling industrial platform built into an abandoned shipping zone beside the river. Cargo cranes towered above rusted docks while relay dishes and armored conduits spread across interconnected rooftops below.

Falcon studied the image carefully. "How do we get close enough without turning the whole district into a firefight?"

Owl expanded another window beside the map. "ARGUS is still monitoring Jay's behavioral profile. We use that."

Jay already understood where the conversation was heading before Eagle spoke again.

"We give ARGUS exactly what it expects to see," Eagle said. "A fracture inside the team."

The room remained quiet.

Finch leaned back in his chair near the tactical console while spinning a data drive between his claws. "A believable argument," he said. "Not screaming. Not theatrical. Just enough tension to convince the system Jay's drifting away from command structure. While ARGUS focuses on that, Owl and I feed false telemetry through the compromised relay channels."

Jay felt the knot tighten in his stomach, though he kept his expression steady.

"If ARGUS thinks I'm unstable," he said, "it shifts resources toward me."

"That's the idea," Falcon replied.

Cardinal looked toward Jay calmly. "The important thing is remembering it's only a performance."

Eagle's eyes rested on Jay for a moment longer than the others.

"Once ARGUS commits to the lie," Eagle said, "we move fast. Falcon leads the strike teams. Owl severs coordination from the Nest. Cardinal anchors extraction. Jay and Finch go for the forward node."

Jay nodded once. "Understood."

The staged argument happened two hours later inside the communications array.

The room hummed softly with signal traffic while technicians pretended not to watch from nearby stations. Jay stood near the central relay table while Eagle faced him from across the chamber.

"You're drifting off mission," Eagle said sharply enough for the monitored channels to capture every word. "You think chasing Harrier matters more than the team."

Jay forced frustration into his expression without letting it become reckless. "You told me to lead. I'm trying to."

"Leadership doesn't mean flying alone."

Owl's eyes flicked briefly toward one of the hidden monitors, silently confirming the signal leak remained active. Finch stood near the back wall feeding subtle telemetry distortions into the compromised channels while pretending to stay focused on calibration work.

Jay stepped forward. "Maybe nobody else is willing to admit we're missing something."

"And maybe," Eagle answered coldly, "you're letting ARGUS steer you exactly where it wants."

The silence afterward felt painfully real despite everyone in the room knowing the argument had been staged.

Then Eagle pointed toward the exit.

"Leave."

Jay stared at him for one long second before turning and walking out of the array room while the monitored channels carried every moment directly into ARGUS's waiting systems.

Falcon spent the rest of the afternoon drilling the operation until every movement felt automatic. By evening, the mission no longer resembled a complicated plan so much as a set of instincts burned directly into muscle memory.

The Nest grew quieter as launch time approached.

Owl tracked relay movement from the operations floor while Finch finalized the Ghost Jay telemetry package in the adjacent lab. Cardinal prepared equipment in near silence, pausing only briefly to murmur a prayer beneath his breath while checking cocoon harnesses one final time.

Jay stood near the hangar overlook watching snow drift across the mountains outside when Finch appeared beside him carrying two steaming cups of coffee balanced awkwardly against one wing.

"You look terrible," Finch announced.

"Thanks."

"You're welcome."

Jay accepted the coffee and leaned against the railing.

For several minutes neither of them spoke. Below them, launch crews moved between the rails preparing strike teams while engines warmed deep inside the mountain.

Finally Finch glanced sideways at him. "You know Eagle almost cracked during the fake argument, right?"

Jay frowned. "What?"

"He hated it," Finch replied. "He just hides it better than the rest of us."

Jay stared back out toward the mountains.

"I know the Harrier stuff is getting inside your head," Finch said more quietly now. "But none of us think you're turning."

Jay looked at him. "You never doubted it?"

Finch snorted softly. "Jaybird, you worry too much about everybody else to become a villain. You'd apologize to the planet while taking it over."

Jay laughed despite himself.

That was Finch's gift. Somehow he always understood exactly when tension inside a room needed to break before it crushed somebody. The sound of Jay laughing seemed to satisfy him more than the joke itself.

"You ready for tonight?" Jay asked.

"No," Finch answered honestly. "But I brought snacks, which is basically emotional preparedness."

The laugh came easier that time.

Below them, Falcon's voice echoed across the hangar.

"Launch teams move."

The moment had arrived.

Dawn spread pale gray light across the river as Blue Team approached the target zone.

The abandoned shipping platform rose from the water ahead of them in layers of steel walkways, relay towers, and weather-stained cargo structures. Radar dishes rotated slowly above the rooftops while thick conduit cables stretched between buildings like webs across the industrial complex.

"ARGUS is watching the feed," Owl said over comms from the Nest. "Ghost Jay telemetry is active."

Eagle's voice followed immediately afterward. "Stay disciplined. We only get one shot at this."

Jay angled downward toward the central platform while Finch followed close behind him, broadcasting the false telemetry package across the monitored channels exactly as planned.

"You don't understand!" Jay shouted into the open comms, letting frustration bleed into his voice. "They already know everything!"

"Jay, break off!" Finch yelled back convincingly. "You're flying straight into a trap!"

Turrets rotated toward them instantly.

The lie had worked.

Black-feathered sentries emerged from the shadows along the platform edges while signal activity spiked violently across Owl's tracking screens back at the Nest.

Jay landed hard against the platform deck and staggered deliberately while Finch dropped beside him.

One of the sentries stepped closer, dark mask gleaming beneath the rising sun.

"You finally understand," the Vulture hissed. "ARGUS already sees the ending."

Overhead speakers crackled softly.

Then another voice rolled across the platform, calm and terrible.

Cipher.

"People fracture predictably," he said. "That is why systems endure longer than loyalty."

Finch leaned close enough for only Jay to hear him.

"Now."

He activated the jammer.

The platform died instantly.

Lights vanished. Screens collapsed. Turrets froze mid-rotation.

Then the Aviary struck.

Falcon crashed through the rooftop defenses in a shower of sparks while Cardinal drove directly into the sentry line hard enough to scatter birds across the deck. Red Team descended behind them through smoke and confusion while Owl flooded Jay's visor with updated routes and structural weak points.

“Move,” Eagle ordered.

Jay and Finch sprinted toward the relay chamber while the battle exploded around them.

Inside the structure, the central node pulsed beneath layers of armored conduits and rotating diagnostic lights. The Egg sat buried inside the relay spine like a heart pumping signal traffic through the entire platform.

Finch slid to the console immediately, claws moving rapidly across the interface.

“Give me thirty seconds.”

“You have twenty.”

“That’s deeply unhelpful.”

Outside, the fight intensified. Metal groaned overhead while alarms screamed across the platform. Through the fractured doorway, Jay caught glimpses of Falcon weaving through turret fire while Cardinal held the main corridor almost alone against a surge of advancing Vultures.

Then the scarred enforcer from the ridge appeared through the smoke.

His red optics locked onto Jay instantly.

“You led them here,” the Vulture growled. “ARGUS predicted every move.”

Jay shifted sideways as the attack came. The enforcer hit hard enough to crack the relay railing beside him apart, but Jay redirected the momentum and drove the Vulture backward into a support column instead.

“You believed your own trap,” Jay shot back.

The Vulture lunged again.

This time Jay pivoted unexpectedly, throwing the strike angle off just enough for the enforcer to miss before crashing into the relay frame.

“Done!” Finch shouted. “Node severed! Cache extracted!”

Owl's voice cut across comms. "We have the data. Extraction now!"

Then the platform spoke.

"Self-destruct sequence initiated."

The voice did not belong to Cipher.

It belonged to ARGUS itself.

Cold. Absolute. Unhurried.

Every alarm on the platform turned red.

Heat surged upward through the relay deck while warning sirens erupted across the structure. Somewhere below them, explosions rolled through the lower supports one after another.

Jay grabbed Finch's harness. "Move!"

They sprinted toward the exit just as the floor buckled violently beneath them.

The explosion threw Jay sideways hard enough to knock the breath from his lungs. Metal screamed overhead while smoke swallowed the corridor.

Then he heard Finch cry out.

Jay spun immediately.

A collapsed support beam pinned Finch beneath twisted steel only a few yards away. One wing lay trapped beneath the wreckage while flames crawled rapidly along the fractured support frame above him.

Jay lunged toward the beam and pulled with everything he had.

It didn't move.

Another explosion shook the platform.

The structure groaned overhead while sparks rained through the smoke.

"Jay," Finch coughed. "Stop."

"No."

Jay pulled again desperately. Pain tore through his shoulders while the beam shifted barely an inch before slamming back down harder than before. Nearby panels flashed evacuation warnings in brutal red countdown numbers.

There wasn't enough time.

Panic hit him hard enough to blur his vision. For one terrible moment he kept pulling blindly anyway, refusing to accept what was happening in front of him.

Then he forced himself to stop long enough to actually look.

The beam had collapsed directly into the main support joint. Moving it the wrong way would bring the entire ceiling down.

Both of them would die.

Jay looked back at Finch.

Finch already knew.

Smoke drifted between them while alarms screamed across the collapsing chamber. Then Finch lifted his wing weakly and transferred the packet cache across their bands.

Jay's display blinked once.

DATA TRANSFER COMPLETE.

"Proof," Finch whispered through a weak, crooked smile, "not guesses."

Jay shook his head violently. "We can still do this."

The evacuation timer continued falling.

Finch looked at him steadily through the smoke. Fear was there now. Jay could finally see it beneath the exhaustion and pain. But underneath the fear sat something stronger.

Trust.

“Hey,” Finch said softly. “Baseball game after this, right?”

Jay felt his throat close instantly.

A hundred memories crashed through him at once. Finch upside down on the rec room couch arguing impossible playoff math. Finch smuggling snacks into briefings. Finch talking too loudly during missions because silence made him nervous. Finch making everybody else laugh whenever tension inside the Nest became unbearable.

“Don’t do this,” Jay whispered.

Finch’s smile trembled slightly. “Then listen carefully.”

Jay’s claws tightened helplessly against the beam.

“Don’t let this thing turn you into somebody cold,” Finch said quietly. “That’s how it wins.”

Another explosion rolled through the platform.

Above them, Falcon’s voice cracked across comms. “Jay, we have to go!”

Jay ignored her completely.

“I’m not leaving you.”

“Yes, you are,” Finch answered, and for one heartbreaking second he sounded calmer than anyone else in the collapsing room. “Because if our places were reversed, you know I’d drag you out myself.”

Jay couldn’t breathe.

Finch looked at him one final time.

“You get everybody home,” he said softly.

Then he shoved Jay backward just as the support frame above them failed completely.

The ceiling collapsed.

Jay launched on instinct as fire exploded through the relay chamber behind him. The blast hurled him violently into open air beyond the platform while heat and smoke swallowed everything underneath.

For several disoriented seconds there was nothing except white heat, deafening noise, and the terrible certainty that Finch was gone.

Then cold air hit him.

He caught himself clumsily and climbed.

Below him, the platform folded inward while flames tore through the relay spine and spread across the river in burning reflections.

"Jay!"

Falcon slid beneath his wing to steady him before he lost altitude again. Cardinal rose on his opposite side moments later, battered but still airborne.

Owl's voice came across comms from the Nest, painfully controlled.

"The packet cache is secure."

Jay tried answering but his throat barely worked.

"We have it," he forced out finally.

Eagle responded after a long silence.

"All units return home."

That was all he said.

No speeches. No attempt to soften what had happened.

Blue Team turned east toward the mountains while smoke rose behind them across the river.

During the flight home, Jay kept waiting for Finch's voice to cut through the comms with some stupid joke about almost dying again. Every burst of static made part of his mind expect it automatically. The silence that followed each time felt wrong in a way Jay could barely process.

Halfway back to the Nest, Owl transmitted a course correction.

Jay didn't react.

Falcon glanced sharply toward him before repeating the adjustment herself.

Only then did Jay realize Finch usually handled navigation confirmations during flights like this. Finch filled dead air. Finch repeated updates. Finch kept everyone moving together.

Now the comms carried nothing except wind noise and clipped operational reports.

The silence felt enormous.

Jay pressed his wrist tightly against his chest during the final stretch home. Finch's last transfer still glowed across the band display beneath layers of mission telemetry and extraction data.

Ahead of them, the mountains slowly emerged through the clouds.

For the first time since joining the Aviary, the formation no longer felt complete.

Chapter 23: Dust to Dust

Dawn came slowly to the Nest.

The hangar doors stood partially open to the mountains, letting cold wind drift across the flight deck while the great American flag above the launch rails moved heavily in the early light. Snow swirled outside the entrance in loose gray sheets, and somewhere deeper in the base engines rumbled at low idle as crews worked through the remains of the night.

Jay landed alone.

His talons scraped hard against the metal deck before he finally stopped moving. The DATA PASS: SECURE marker still blinked faintly across his wrist display, but he barely looked at it anymore. His claw remained wrapped instead around the small tool-bit Finch had carried everywhere, the one marked with faded powder-blue tape that somehow always seemed to end up fixing broken things.

Now it was all Jay had left to hold.

Eagle, Falcon, Cardinal, and Owl waited near the edge of the deck. None of them rushed toward him. None of them tried to fill the silence with comforting words that wouldn't help anyway.

Jay finally looked up, eyes raw from smoke and exhaustion.

“It should’ve been me.”

The words came out quieter than he intended.

Eagle stepped forward first. “No,” he said evenly. “Finch made a choice.”

Jay shook his head immediately. “I could’ve gotten him out.”

“You would’ve died with him,” Falcon answered softly.

Jay looked away from them toward the mountains outside the hangar. The horizon had begun turning pale gold behind the clouds, but he felt strangely detached from it, as though the world had continued moving while some part of him remained trapped inside the collapsing relay chamber beside Finch.

Cardinal rested a wing gently against his shoulder. “You came home carrying what he protected,” he said. “That matters.”

Jay tightened his grip around the taped tool-bit until the metal edge dug painfully into his claw.

“It doesn’t feel like enough.”

Nobody argued with him.

That hurt more than reassurance would have.

At sunrise they raised the flag to half-staff.

The entire Nest gathered quietly along the flight deck and mezzanine rails while mountain wind rolled through the open hangar. Maintenance crews stood beside pilots. Analysts stood beside mechanics. Even the younger trainees who barely understood the full scope of the war had fallen silent.

Cardinal led the prayer.

He didn’t speak loudly, and he didn’t try to make the moment grander than it already was.

"Lord, receive your son," he said quietly. "Grant us courage for the work ahead and wisdom enough to protect the peace he gave his life for."

The words drifted through the hangar while the flag climbed slowly upward before stopping midway against the morning sky.

A single bugle note echoed out across the canyon.

Nobody moved.

Jay stood beside the Wall of the Fallen long after the others stepped back. Owl quietly slid a slim data drive beneath Finch's newly engraved nameplate while Falcon lowered her head beside the wall with both wings folded tightly against her sides.

The drive still carried Finch's handwritten label across the top.

don't crash pls —F

Jay stared at it for several seconds before carefully placing the powder-blue tool-bit beneath the edge of the plaque so that a strip of the tape remained visible.

Like Finch was still somewhere nearby, leaving pieces of himself behind on purpose.

"He would've hated everybody standing around looking this sad," Falcon muttered after a while.

A weak laugh escaped Jay before he could stop it.

"Yeah," he said quietly. "He would've made a joke by now."

Owl looked toward the plaque. "He never stopped transmitting during the collapse."

Jay swallowed hard.

Even at the end, Finch had kept working.

The next ten days passed in constant motion.

The war did not end all at once. It unraveled.

Owl coordinated strike routes from the operations floor while Falcon led teams against the remaining relay sites scattered across the country. Some operations targeted abandoned infrastructure hidden beneath cities. Others intercepted dormant Eggs before they could reconnect to surviving ARGUS fragments.

Jay flew nearly all of them.

Not recklessly.
Not angrily.

Differently.

He spoke less during missions now. He listened longer before making decisions. When younger pilots panicked during turbulence or rushed through approach routes, Jay corrected them calmly instead of sharply. More than once he caught himself repeating small habits Finch used to make fun of, like double-checking every cocoon seal personally before launch or carrying extra ration packs because somebody always forgot theirs.

The changes came quietly enough that he barely noticed them at first.

Others did.

During one relief mission in the Midwest, Blue Team escorted emergency crews into a town where winter storms had knocked out power for nearly three days. Jay helped guide supply trucks through collapsed streets while Cardinal organized warming shelters inside an old school gymnasium. Falcon repaired a damaged rooftop antenna with two exhausted local linemen while Owl stabilized emergency communications from the back of a utility vehicle.

Late that night, after the generators finally came back online, a little girl approached Jay near the shelter entrance carrying a flashlight almost as long as her wing.

“My mom said you fixed the lights,” she said.

Jay looked down at the flashlight, then at the glowing school windows behind her.

“Not by myself,” he answered.

The girl nodded seriously, as though that mattered very much.

Before leaving, she handed him a folded paper drawing of several birds flying above the school beneath a badly uneven yellow sun.

One of the birds wore oversized goggles.

Jay nearly lost himself right there in the parking lot.

Instead, he folded the drawing carefully and slid it into the pouch beside Finch’s tool-bit.

The Nest slowly changed with the missions.

Damaged hangars were repaired. New trainees arrived. The younger teams began learning how to identify relay contamination before it spread. Owl converted one of the lower briefing rooms into a permanent monitoring center for dormant ARGUS fragments while Falcon rebuilt the field training courses to focus less on combat and more on civilian extraction and infrastructure defense.

“Most wars aren’t won by blowing things up,” she told a room full of trainees one afternoon while Jay watched from the back wall. “They’re won by keeping people alive long enough to rebuild afterward.”

Jay noticed several of the younger birds looking toward him now before exercises started, waiting for confirmation before moving.

At first the attention made him uncomfortable.

Then he understood what Finch had seen long before he did.

Leadership inside the Aviary was never about sounding fearless.

It was about being the bird others looked toward when things became uncertain.

One evening Eagle found Jay alone on the upper observation deck overlooking the mountains.

Snow drifted quietly beyond the railings while the lights of the Nest glowed beneath them through the stone.

"You've changed," Eagle said.

Jay rested his arms against the cold metal railing. "Losing Finch changed all of us."

"Yes," Eagle answered. "But grief hardens some birds. You've let it sharpen you instead."

Jay looked down at the powder-blue tape wrapped around the tool-bit in his claw.

"I still hear him during missions sometimes."

Eagle nodded once. "Good."

Jay glanced sideways toward him.

"You don't honor birds like Finch by pretending the loss disappears," Eagle said quietly. "You honor them by carrying forward the parts of them worth saving."

Wind rolled softly across the overlook.

Below them, training teams crossed the lower launch deck while maintenance crews prepared transports for another overnight relief operation farther south.

The work never really stopped now.

And somehow that helped.

Spring arrived slowly in the mountains.

The final memorial flight happened on a clear morning beneath enormous blue skies stretching far beyond the ridgelines. Every active Aviary unit assembled above the Nest while recovery crews, analysts, technicians, and trainees watched from the decks below.

Jay flew near the front formation now.

Not because Eagle ordered it.

Because over time the position had simply become his.

As the formation climbed higher above the mountains, Falcon moved into place along his right side while Cardinal settled to his left. Owl flew slightly above them, steady and watchful against the bright morning sky. Behind the formation, Eagle held the rear center position with quiet certainty.

One space remained open.

Nobody filled it.

The wind moved cold and clean across Jay's feathers while the formation turned east into the rising sunlight. Far below them, the Nest had already resumed its ordinary rhythm. Supply flights launched from the lower hangars. Rescue crews trained across the western cliffs. Rebuilding missions prepared for departure.

Life continued.

Jay looked once toward the empty space beside the formation.

Finch should have been there complaining about the temperature or talking too loudly over comms or insisting he had secretly become the best flyer on the team.

Instead there was only open sky.

The ache of that would probably never leave him completely.

But as Jay climbed higher with the team around him and the mountains falling away below, he realized something else had survived alongside the grief.

Not just duty.

Not just responsibility.

Hope.

And for the first time since the relay platform collapsed into fire beneath the river, Jay no longer felt like he was flying toward a war.

He felt like he was helping build whatever came after it.

Epilogue: A Legacy of Feathers

The Nest, One Year Later.

Spring had finally reached the mountains.

Warm air drifted through the open flight deck of the Nest carrying the scent of thawing earth, pine, and wet stone. Far below the canyon walls, meltwater rushed through narrow streams that had been frozen solid only weeks earlier. The mountain no longer felt like a fortress preparing for war. It felt alive again.

Jay stood near the edge of the platform with his wings folded loosely at his sides while the morning wind moved through his feathers.

A year had changed him.

His shoulders had broadened. The sharp urgency that once followed him everywhere had settled into something steadier now. The electric-blue trim along his flight harness had faded from weather and real operations, and a pale scar still crossed the inside of his right wing joint from Istanbul. Sometimes it tightened during storms. Mostly it just reminded him how far back the road behind him stretched now.

In his talons, he turned a weathered feather carefully between his claws.

Finch's feather.

The same one he had caught during twilight a year earlier.

Behind him, the Nest had already begun its morning rhythm. New recruits crossed the training deck in uneven formations while instructors corrected spacing and timing beneath the canyon walls. Some struggled through turbulence drills above the western cliffs while others worked through observation exercises inside the lower range rooms where Owl monitored every rushed decision with ruthless patience.

The tech bay doors stood open nearby.

Above them hung a simple metal sign:

FINCH LAB

Every toolbox inside carried a thin strip of yellow tape somewhere along the handle or casing. None of it matched perfectly. Some strips were bright and fresh while others had already begun peeling at the corners.

No one had ordered it.
No one removed them either.

Some of the younger recruits probably didn't even know why the tape mattered anymore.

They just knew it did.

Jay watched a pair of trainees hurry past the bay carrying signal equipment almost too large for them. One nearly dropped a case before the other caught it at the last second.

"Easy," the second recruit laughed. "You break Owl's equipment, she'll recycle your soul."

Jay smiled faintly before looking back toward the horizon.

The war against ARGUS had ended months earlier, but the work left behind by it hadn't disappeared so easily. The Aviary still flew patrol routes every day. Recovery crews still searched for dormant relay systems buried beneath cities and coastlines. Some missions delivered emergency power systems to damaged towns. Others tracked scattered

Vulture cells that surfaced briefly before disappearing again into the noise of the world.

Most days were quieter now.

But not simple.

Footsteps approached behind him.

Eagle stepped beside the railing without speaking at first. Time had not diminished him. If anything, it had sharpened the calm steadiness he carried into every room. The white feathers along his crown caught the morning sunlight while the deep lines near his eyes looked earned rather than aged.

For a while they simply watched the younger recruits crossing the canyon airspace below.

One formation drifted too wide near the southern ridge.

“Too loose,” Jay said automatically.

Eagle glanced sideways toward him. “You noticed before the instructor did.”

Jay shrugged slightly. “Crosswinds near the ridge push younger flyers outward. They’re overcorrecting.”

“And what would you tell them?”

Jay watched the formation recover unevenly before answering.

“Slow down before adjusting. Most mistakes get worse because birds panic halfway through fixing them.”

Eagle nodded once, satisfied.

The silence between them remained comfortable.

Jay rolled Finch’s feather slowly between his claws. “He would’ve loved this.”

"Yes," Eagle answered quietly. "He would."

Jay looked down toward the flight deck where a broad-shouldered recruit had somehow gathered a crowd around himself near the supply carts.

Pelican.

Even from a distance he was impossible to miss.

His oversized utility belt bounced wildly against his sides while he waddled in exaggerated slow motion across the deck carrying three equipment crates stacked far above his head.

"Now if any of y'all panic during turbulence," Pelican announced gravely to the younger recruits around him, "remember to flap calm and panic polite."

The recruits burst into laughter.

Then the launch buzzer sounded.

The transformation happened instantly.

Pelican dropped the crates into place, squared his stance, and launched from the deck in one smooth motion that erased every trace of clumsiness. His heavy wings cut through the canyon air with surprising precision as he rolled cleanly into a steep attack profile above the target range.

A practice charge dropped from beneath his harness.

Dead center.

The younger recruits erupted again.

Jay shook his head with a quiet smile. "Finch would've adopted him immediately."

"Probably fed him too much sugar," Eagle replied.

Nearby, another blur shot through the lower timing course so quickly that sunlight flashed green and violet across her feathers only in brief streaks.

Hummingbird.

Small.
Fast.
Impossible to track once she accelerated.

She landed lightly on the edge of the course platform already scanning the next obstacle before her claws fully settled.

Above her, Crow watched from a narrow support beam bolted high against the canyon wall. Matte-black feathers blended into the steel shadows around him so completely that most recruits never noticed him until he moved. He rarely spoke during training sessions. He simply observed everything with unnerving patience.

The next generation was forming around them.

Different personalities.
Different strengths.
Same purpose.

Jay felt the weight of that more now than he once would have.

A year earlier he had thought leadership meant being the strongest bird in the room.

Now he understood it meant helping everyone else survive long enough to become strong themselves.

The realization had cost him more than he would ever fully explain.

A soft tone chimed through his wrist comm.

Owl.

“Jay,” she said calmly. “You near a console?”

“On the overlook. Why?”

A brief pause answered him first.

“While clearing the final ARGUS archives,” Owl said carefully, “I found a transmission buried beneath several corrupted relay layers. Recent. Masked heavily.”

Jay’s posture straightened immediately.

“What identifier?”

Another pause.

Then:

“Harrier.”

The wind seemed colder suddenly.

Jay tightened his grip around the feather.

“That’s impossible.”

“Unlikely,” Owl corrected. “But the signal triangulated consistently before it vanished.”

“Where?”

“The Scottish Highlands.”

Jay stared out toward the horizon without really seeing it anymore.

No Vulture activity. No active ARGUS network. No relay chatter.

Just a signal.

A whisper.

Somewhere deep inside him, something shifted quietly back into motion.

Harrier.

His father.
His mystery.
The unfinished wound sitting underneath everything else.

Jay lowered his gaze toward the deck below where Pelican was now arguing loudly with a maintenance drone while Hummingbird timed recruits through another launch sequence.

Life continued.

Training continued.
Repairs continued.
The Aviary continued.

And still the thread tugged.

Without fully thinking about it, Jay opened a private map layer across his wrist display and marked a remote point in the Highlands.

CAIRN-7

He stared at the waypoint for several seconds.

Then he set a pre-dawn departure alarm.

Canceled it.

Stood there another moment.

Set it again.

Beside him, Eagle said nothing.

He simply rested both talons against the railing and looked out over the canyon while the younger recruits crossed the morning sky below them in messy, determined formations.

Far beyond the mountains, storms rolled across distant sea cliffs where waves hammered ancient black stone beneath the night.

Lightning flashed briefly across a hidden hangar carved deep into the rock.

Inside, darkness shifted.

Old machinery hummed faintly beneath layers of dust while damaged monitors flickered weak green light across rusted floors and hanging cables. A torn Vulture banner swayed gently near the back wall where cold wind slipped through cracks in the stone.

Somewhere deeper inside the structure, metal scraped slowly against rock.

A lens flickered awake.

Then another.

And in the darkness beyond the catwalks, something began moving again.

About the Author

Matthew Martin is an American author and executive whose career has been devoted to preserving history and building the future. As a leader in architectural preservation, he has overseen the restoration of historic landmarks across the United States, blending craftsmanship, strategy, and disciplined execution. His professional life has been rooted in safeguarding legacy—ensuring that the stories told in stone, plaster, and paint endure for generations.

A former professional performer with Riverdance, Matthew brings a deep appreciation for rhythm, legacy, and tradition into his storytelling. Years of international performance instilled in him a respect for precision, teamwork, and the power of shared purpose—elements that now shape both his leadership and his fiction.

His writing reflects a lifelong fascination with courage, loyalty, sacrifice, and the fragile balance between order and freedom. Drawing inspiration from history, service, and the enduring spirit of American ideals, he crafts stories that explore what it truly costs to defend what matters most.

The Aviary: Rise of the Wings is the first installment in his debut trilogy, a near-future military thriller exploring liberty, leadership, and the weight of responsibility in an age of technological power.

Born into a military family in San Diego, California, Matthew now lives in New Jersey with his wife, Colleen, and their two children, Nolan and Evie, where he continues to imagine the next flight of the Aviary.

www.ingramcontent.com/pod-product-compliance
Lightning Source LLC
LaVergne TN
LVHW090514110826
845146LV00003B/852

* 9 7 9 8 2 3 4 0 1 9 8 6 8 *